"You've _____
me, h _____

"No," Lindsay said slowly. "Not always. When I first went to work for you, I...I admired you very much." He didn't need to hear how everyone had drooled over him, the good-looking tycoon who ruled from the regal splendor of the tenth floor. The day Daniel brought his daughter to a board meeting, for instance, had been the stuff of legend.

"So when did all that change?" Daniel's gaze had never faltered from her face.

She raised her glass in a mocking salute. "Well, you *did* fire me, remember?"

KATHLEEN O'BRIEN, who lives in Florida, started out as a newspaper feature writer, but after marriage and motherhood, she traded that in to work on a novel. Kathleen likes strong heroes who overcome adversity, which is probably the result of her reading—when she was younger—all those classic novels featuring tragic heroes. However, being a true romantic, she prefers *her* stories to end happily!

Books by Kathleen O'Brien

If you like strong emotion and sizzling intensity in your romances, you'll love MISTLETOE MAN—the latest from talented author Kathleen O'Brien!

KATHLEEN O'BRIEN

Mistletoe Man

Harlequin Books

TORONTO • NEW YORK • LONDON
AMSTERDAM • PARIS • SYDNEY • HAMBURG
STOCKHOLM • ATHENS • TOKYO • MILAN
MADRID • WARSAW • BUDAPEST • AUCKLAND

ISBN 0-373-11853-8

MISTLETOE MAN

First North American Publication 1996.

CHAPTER ONE

LINDSAY BLAISDELL held her breath as the helicopter
hit another air pocket, dipping and tilting like a carnival
ride. Groaning as its metal belly missed a treetop by
inches, she shut her eyes miserably. What on God's earth
was she doing up here? She'd always detested flying, even
in a comfortable jumbo jet. But flying through a snowstorm in a tiny, cruelly cold helicopter, just for the joy
of meeting with the arrogant Mr. Daniel McKinley—well,
that was torture in a class by itself.

And, to put it bluntly, he wasn't worth it. She hadn't
seen the man in three years, but she hadn't forgotten
him. The thirty-ish wunderkind president of the
McKinley Corporation, he'd been smart, stubborn and,
at six-foot-two with curling black hair and icy blue eyes,
perhaps justifiably self-satisfied. He had been a ruthless
businessman, a relentless boss and, by all accounts, a
wretched husband. No candidate for sainthood. Not even
for the local Mr. Nice Guy.

All in all, she thought bitterly as the helicopter dipped
again, he darn sure wasn't worth dying for.

Snowy treetops lunged toward her, their branches
reaching with white, grasping fingers, and the pilot let
loose a manic chuckle, as if he and the wind were en-
gaged in a friendly wrestling match. Just the kind of
can-do, zealous overachiever Lindsay would have expected Daniel McKinley to employ. Reluctantly the pilot
righted the copter at the last minute, having avoided a
crash by approximately the breadth of two snowflakes.

5

As the horizon straightened out, Lindsay swallowed
the acrid taste of her morning coffee—which hadn't even
tasted all that great going down—and relaxed her hold
on the briefcase she clutched against her pounding heart.
When she felt reasonably sure she wasn't going to be ill,
she decided that she hated two things above all others:
helicopters, and helicopter pilots who thought near-death
experiences were exhilarating.

"There it is," the pilot yelled over the roar of the rotor.
He jabbed his forefinger earthward, still grinning.
"McKinley's place."

Lindsay peered down and, as the treetops thinned out,
a redwood ski lodge appeared just twenty yards below
them. McKinley's place. Massive, elegant and handsome,
it claimed this mountain with a silent dominance.

Handsome. Elegant. Domineering. Why did that
sound more like McKinley himself than his house?
Perhaps, she mused, there *was* something she hated more
than daredevil pilots. She hated arrogant men who sat,
enthroned in mountain fortresses, expecting the world
to come to them. Even when the weather was wicked
and unwelcoming. Even when it was nearly Christmas,
and he had to realize that most people wanted to be at
home, wrapping presents by the fire.

Suddenly, shoved by an invisible gust, the copter
lurched sideways, and branches made awful screeching
sounds against the window. Lindsay started and, looking
over, saw that the pilot's grin had flattened out. He
gripped the controls tightly, fighting the currents that
buffeted his little craft.

"Is everything okay?" she asked. The question was
pointless, and the pilot didn't bother to answer her. She
held her breath again as the helicopter began its wob-
bling descent. The winds were much stronger now than
when they had left Denver's little executive airfield. She

hoped this guy was at least half as good as he thought he was.

It seemed to take forever, but finally the helicopter found the ground. It rocked crazily as it landed, like a top bobbling to a stop, and when the motion ceased both pilot and passenger sat speechless, breathing deeply, staring wordlessly at the silent, dark lodge before them.

After a long moment the pilot finally spoke. "Pretty damn bleak, ain't it? Don't know what in hell anyone would want to come here for this time of year."

Lindsay had no answer for that. She didn't know, either. She certainly wouldn't have come here by choice. The house did look bleak, its roof shrouded in white, snow creeping up the corners in wind-driven drifts. Dead, almost. As if it waited for someone who would never come back.

But then she shook herself, annoyed. A "dead" house, indeed! She was imagining things simply because she knew about the tragedy that had occurred here three years ago.

No, the only reason this house was so silent was that Daniel McKinley, for all his wealth, didn't have enough manners to come outside to greet his guest.

Scowling, she unhooked her seat belt. He hadn't changed at all, had he? He had always been a heartless son of a gun. Didn't he know the weather had turned nasty? If he didn't care about *her* safety, wasn't he at least concerned about whether his expensive copter-toy might have wrapped itself around a Douglas fir?

Suddenly the double doors of the lodge opened, and two men emerged onto the wide front porch. Lindsay peered through the dim light, but the swirling white air was like bad reception on a television set, and all she could see were two tall, male figures. Frustrated, she opened the door and slid out, sinking ankle deep in snow and dropping her briefcase as she tried to steady herself.

"Curses!" She knew stronger words, gratifying Germanic words that would have fit the occasion much better, but she had long ago trained herself, for Christy's sake, not to use them. She bent over to retrieve the case, dragging her coat hem through the snow. It was old snow, *wet* snow, she discovered, lifting the briefcase and the coat simultaneously. A very cold, very slushy snow. "Double-dog-curse the man."

By the time she was fully upright again, her hair was sticking to her cheeks, and one of the men she had seen on the porch was standing at her side. "Can I help you?" His voice was solicitous, with a hint of a Southern accent, and she knew instantly that it wasn't Daniel McKinley. She'd never forget the deep timbre of McKinley's voice.

"Gosh, I'm sorry," the man was saying. "If we'd known it was you . . . I mean that you were a woman . . ." He sounded flustered, and he fumbled for her briefcase, nearly dropping his own case in the process. "I mean, Daniel said he was expecting someone named Robert."

Lindsay tried to ignore the anxiety that surfaced at his words. It was true, of course. Daniel had, quite rightly, been expecting Robert Hamilton, owner of Hamilton Homes, to be on this helicopter. She knew Daniel wouldn't be pleased to have to deal with a mere assistant in Robert's place. And when he found out who the assistant was, when he found out it was Lindsay . . .

But that couldn't be helped now. She peeled a hank of half-frozen hair from the edge of her mouth and swallowed a lump of cold air as the second man—Daniel himself—began walking toward the helicopter. Her fingers twitched nervously inside her gloves.

"Daniel!" The man at her side sounded amused. "Your guest has arrived, but I'm afraid it's no Robert." He tilted his head at Lindsay. "Perhaps a Roberta?"

"Lindsay," she corrected, but her voice was husky, nervous. She cleared her throat.

"Roberta Lindsay?" The man's smile broadened.

Lindsay shook her head. "No," she said, trying to read Daniel's expression through the snow, trying to see if he recognized her. "Lindsay Blaisdell." She squared her shoulders and put out her gloved hand. "Hello, Mr. McKinley."

"Miss Blaisdell. What a pleasant surprise." But he didn't look surprised—he didn't even look annoyed, which he must have been, especially if he connected *this* Lindsay Blaisdell with the one he had fired three years ago. But of course, like all good businessmen, he was a master at hiding his emotions.

"Robert wasn't able to come after all," she began, already absurdly defensive, especially considering she was answering a question he hadn't even asked. "He's not here."

Daniel smiled. "Evidently," he said mildly. He turned to the man with the briefcase. "Well, I think we did a good day's work, Steve. I trust you'll have a smooth trip back. Wind's up, but my pilot is very good."

"He's very sick," Lindsay was surprised to hear herself speaking again, but Daniel's indifference to her presence was somehow galling and she felt an overwhelming urge to make him notice her. How dare he turn his back on her? "His appendix burst."

Daniel turned slowly, dark brows raised over his quizzical blue gaze. "My pilot?"

Lindsay flushed. He'd noticed her, all right. Noticed her making a fool of herself. She had always felt gauche and tongue-tied around Daniel McKinley, but, darn it, she'd been only twenty then, and ridiculously innocent. Besides, he had no power over her anymore. She didn't work for him. He couldn't just summarily fire her for making a stupid comment. He'd already done that.

"No, of course not your pilot," she said quickly, nearly stammering anyway. "Robert." When he still looked quizzical, she tried again. "Mr. Hamilton."

"Yes, of course." He was smiling again, and she knew he was making fun of her. "Mr. Hamilton, who isn't here." He reached across her shoulder to open the helicopter door. "You must tell me all the details as soon as we get inside. But first we have to get Steve in the air. He has a closing in Denver in less than an hour."

She backed out of the way, biting her lips together to keep from saying anything else idiotic, and watched with mute envy as Steve climbed into the chopper. Taking her elbow, Daniel eased her back even farther as the rotor began to turn, whipping the snow into a frenzy of white, stinging needles. He kept his hand on her arm, and for an uncomfortable moment, as she watched the helicopter rise through the trees, his grip felt like a chain, holding her hostage here, alone with him in this godforsaken outland.

At the last minute Steve waved, his gloved salute barely visible through the thickening snow. And then he was gone. Free. She listened to the disappearing whine of the copter with a sinking heart. Whoever Steve was, wherever he was going, she suddenly would have given a month's pay to trade places with him.

The fire was huge, dancing orange and red inside a stone hearth that must have been twelve feet across, and deliciously hot. Lindsay sat quite close to it, wriggling her tingling fingers and toes nervously, and surveyed the room into which Daniel McKinley had just escorted her.

It was really three rooms, she saw—a living room, with the cushioned couch in front of the fire, where she now sat thawing; an office, with the intricately carved desk on which Daniel had perched to reach Robert's paperwork; and a dining room, with a table big enough to seat twelve comfortably.

It was intensely masculine, yet somehow beautiful. Though the room was at least fifty by sixty, she estimated, soft throw rugs with colorful Indian designs spanned the distances easily. On either side of the hearth, huge windows made a picture postcard of the snowy mountainside, and over in the corner a scented Jacuzzi hummed and bubbled.

The fire dominated all of it, casting its warm, amber glow over deep brown wood floors, beamed ceilings, paneled walls, carved banisters. Even the rich mahogany furniture seemed to be alive with the hint of moving light, creating a surprising sense of intimacy.

Surprising, she thought, and unwelcome.

Intimacy, however brief, with Daniel McKinley was not on her Christmas wish list. And it undoubtedly wasn't on his, either...if men like him ever indulged in such nonsense. He had been courteous but remote as he walked her in, sat her by the fire, poured her a cup of coffee, inquired about her comfort. He had never mentioned the awkward fact that she had once worked for him. But of course he remembered. The fury she'd seen in his eyes the day he had fired her wasn't likely to die in three short years.

No, she didn't wish for intimacy—just for a clean conclusion to the negotiations that had brought her here. And, of course, she wished that he would get off the telephone.

It was driving her crazy to see him sitting on the edge of the desk, the telephone hooked between his ear and shoulder, leafing idly, distractedly, through the loan securitization documents, which she knew were the most important papers she had delivered. It was in those documents that he would find his answer: would he buy Hamilton Homes, thereby saving poor Robert's neck...or would he decide to let his option expire?

But the blasted telephone wouldn't stop ringing. She had to fight the urge to walk over and unplug the cord from the wall jack. She'd been here thirty minutes, her nerves on edge, mentally rehearsing the lines that would surely persuade Daniel that, in spite of the iffy deals Robert had cut, he could, should, *must,* buy Hamilton Homes. All in vain. Of those thirty minutes, Daniel had probably spent twenty-eight on the phone.

"Sorry," he said as, finally concluding the call, he dropped the handset back into its cradle. He had said that five times now, after every interruption.

"That's all right." Her answering murmur wasn't quite as gracious as it had been the first couple of times. Over the past thirty minutes the view through the massive picture windows had grown steadily more opaque, thick with snow. Tall pines were tossing fretfully, bullied by ever-stronger winds. It made her feel slightly sick to think of getting back into that little helicopter.

"Mr. McKinley," she began, emboldened by her sense of urgency. If the winds kept growing more and more intense, would even Daniel's wildman pilot dare to fly? "Mr. McKinley, I'd be glad to answer any questions you might—"

A loud noise interrupted the flow of words, and her voice strangled on a shocked gasp as suddenly, from some hidden recess in the rear of the lodge, a huge, glowering man dressed all in black appeared in front of the fire. Her throat went dry. Who—? She had been so sure that she and Daniel were the only two people left on this snowswept mountain.

For a moment the stranger just stood there, his oversize features shifting eerily in the shadows cast by the fire. Lindsay swallowed hard, staring in spite of herself. He was very old, she sensed, though still a giant of a man. His pronounced, overhanging brows were wild and white, and his hair, which tumbled nearly to his shoulders, was as colorless as the snow.

A flashing glint caught Lindsay's eye, and she dropped her numbed gaze to the man's hands. But, on the left side, there was no hand. Instead, just beyond the intense black of his work shirt, a metal hook glistened in the firelight, sharply curved and lethal.

She was glad she was sitting down, because suddenly the muscles in her legs went limp. She looked toward Daniel, too stunned to speak.

To her surprise he was smiling. "This better be important, Roc." His voice was stern, but it was a mock severity. He flipped one of the document's pages over casually and kept reading while he talked. "Look at Miss Blaisdell's white knuckles. She's frustrated by all these interruptions, I deduce, and holding on to her temper with a superhuman effort. She's eager to finish this deal and get back to civilization."

The huge man turned his glower in Lindsay's direction. "Sick of you already, is she? Well, it'll curdle her guts to hear *my* news, then." He turned back to Daniel. "Landwer called. Seems your chopper's got a rattle, and he's scared to fly until he finds out where it's coming from." He lifted his hook and scratched behind his ear disgustedly. "Yellow-belly wimp-guts."

"Roc, you really are an animal." Settling the papers onto his lap, Daniel shook his head. "My apologies, Miss Blaisdell. Mr. Richter here is my caretaker, and I suspect he's been alone in the wilderness far too long. He's discarded what few manners he ever had.''

But Lindsay wasn't even thinking about the man's rough language. She was too horrified by his message. ''There's something wrong with the helicopter? It's not coming back?'' She stood up, her hands still twisted together, and went to the window, as if she might be able to summon the absent vehicle herself.

But, of course, all she saw was the ever thicker curtain of snow. She turned. ''Mr... Roc,'' she said as steadily as she could. ''Did the pilot say how long it would take to find the problem?''

The big man guffawed. Reaching his good hand out, he grabbed a poker and gave the firewood a rough stirring. The flames roared to new life.

''Don't hold your breath. Landwer couldn't find his rump with a compass.''

''Roc.'' This time Daniel's voice was pitched low and held an unmistakable reprimand.

The giant grinned, and the sight transformed his ugly face into something surprisingly sweet. ''Sorry, Danny Boy, but it's true. If the lady flew up here with him she already knows what a baggage-smasher he is. Don't worry, miss,'' he added with another of his amazing smiles. ''I'll fix something special for dinner to make it easier to stomach old Daniel here.''

''Dinner?'' Lindsay's voice rose. ''But, Mr. McKinley, I have to get back before that. My sister... Christy's too young to be alone.'' She took a deep breath. She mustn't panic. There had to be a way out of this mess. She racked her brain. ''Don't you have another helicopter?''

Daniel smiled wryly. ''Sorry. We're just a one-chopper operation up here. Chintzy, I know, but somehow we've limped by so far.''

"But there must be a car? Or a truck or something?"

"We do have a Jeep," Roc began, but Daniel interrupted, slapping the documents down on the desk crisply.

"No driving," he said. "It's too dangerous. Besides, Landwer will probably have the rattle vanquished in no time. Don't accept Roc's estimate of my pilot's abilities, Miss Blaisdell. Roc used to fly for me before his accident, and he's never been very charitable toward his replacement."

Roc was obviously insulted. He stuffed the poker back into its rack with a terrible clatter. "Listen, Danny Boy, you know bloody well you'd be better off with a couple of carrier pigeons. But what do I care? You and Landwer deserve each other. Anyhow, the Jeep's ready to go, like it is every winter. I could take her—"

"I said no driving." Daniel's earlier lighthearted irony was conspicuously absent. "Go into the kitchen and fix us a good lunch, Roc. Miss Blaisdell will leave when Landwer has repaired the copter. Not before."

Roc left the room as quietly as he came, allowing his anger to show only in the rigidity of his broad back. Lindsay, who had been watching the astonishing interchange in silence, finally moved forward. What an infuriating man Daniel McKinley was! His tone couldn't have been more peremptory if both she and Roc had been his children.

"Mr. McKinley, I really do have to be home before dark tonight. My sister is only twelve years old, and I haven't made any provisions for her care—"

Daniel shrugged one broad shoulder toward the desk. "Feel free to use the telephone."

Lindsay narrowed her eyes. "There's no one to call. I must get home before tonight."

Daniel unfolded himself from the desk, his movements slow and full of coiled, repressed power. His blue eyes were icier than ever.

"You'll leave when I say it's safe, Miss Blaisdell." He looked her up and down, as if assessing her capacity for resistance. "Look, let's get a couple of things straight. Your boss insisted on this eleventh-hour document delivery, not I. I was content to wait until the new year to purchase Hamilton Homes. I will, in point of fact, survive perfectly well if I don't buy Hamilton Homes at all." He met her gaze directly. "Which is more than we can say for your boss, isn't it?"

"That's not the point," she began, but he raised a finger to quiet her words.

"It's the truth," he said. "Now let's be even more honest, shall we? You don't like me. I remember our last encounter with crystal clarity, and I'm well aware that you'd prefer to be anywhere but here. However, here you are, and you must have known the risk you were taking. Winter in these mountains is notorious. If you've been caught by it, we'll just both have to live with that."

Her cheeks were burning, but she refused to be intimidated. "My sister needs me, Mr. McKinley," she repeated stubbornly. "I don't think you understand—"

"No, damn it, it's *you* who doesn't understand." He put his hand on her back and with a rough motion turned her toward the picture window. "Look out there. We have a path that leads to Roc's apartments. It's newly paved, and it's lined with tulips in the spring. Can you see it? Can you even begin to guess where it is?"

She looked, desperately scanning the blank white ripples of mounded snow for anything that resembled a path, but she could find nothing.

"No, of course you can't." She tried to turn away, but his palm was still hard against her back, forcing her to face the window. She didn't dare to speak. He suddenly seemed so intense, almost angry, and she wasn't sure why. Was it because they had finally mentioned the past, that day three years ago when she had uttered one unforgivable sentence?

"You have no idea how treacherous this pretty snow can be," he said, his voice deeper now, almost hypnotic. "It distorts distances, erases landmarks. Take one wrong step, and you can sink into a pocket ten feet deep. Lose your way once, for even ten seconds, and it's virtually impossible to reorient yourself."

"But Roc would be driving," she said quietly. "We'd be in a car."

"Roc is seventy-four years old, Miss Blaisdell, and he has one hand. He's hardly anyone's superhero. You could drive in circles until you run out of gas and then walk in circles until you're so exhausted you can't think straight."

"But—"

"Would that help your little sister?" He lifted her hand, lightly squeezing her fingertips between his thumb and forefinger. The nerves tingled, and a rapid pulse tripped against the pressure. "In fifteen minutes your hands and feet would be numb." He lifted her hand and cupped it against her cheek. "You wouldn't be able to feel your own face."

She shivered suddenly, thinking of that bitter cold, of fingers that would never again feel such warmth as this...

He dropped his hand. "And then you would die, Miss Blaisdell. It's as simple and as terrible as that."

She turned, but, looking at him, she suddenly didn't know what to say. His full mouth was downturned and weary. His eyes looked haunted, seeming to stare right through her. And finally she knew what he had really been talking about. Not her death, but another's. Another car that had foolishly tried to leave this mountain during a blinding, numbing snowstorm. A car that hadn't, horribly, been found for two whole days. A car that, when found, had held the frozen bodies of a beautiful woman and her little girl...

"I'm sorry," Lindsay said, her throat thick and aching with emotions she had no right to express. No right, really, even to feel. "Of course you're right. I'll stay."

Roc brought them lunch in the office area, and while they ate the surprisingly delicious fare—a light, creamy soup and a platter full of fresh fruits and hunks of cheese—Daniel finished studying the documents pertaining to Hamilton Homes.

Lindsay and Roc chatted quietly while Daniel read. Within a very few minutes, Lindsay found herself growing accustomed to Roc's odd looks and earthy language. She even forgot about his hook, until, with a twinkling wink, he speared the last chunk of cheddar cheese with it and plopped it into his mouth. Lindsay blinked, and then, as if he'd done something quite clever, both of them laughed out loud.

Daniel looked up, frowning, his concentration broken, but Roc just laughed harder. "Go back to your homework, Danny Boy. Can't you tell the lady and I are busy?"

And with no more than a wry twist of his mouth, Daniel did just that. Lindsay tried to relax. Roc was so natural, so uninhibited, treating Lindsay, whom he had known for approximately an hour, exactly the same way he treated Daniel—it really was impossible not to like him.

Daniel was another matter. Lindsay kept sneaking glances at him, wondering what he thought of the financial details he was learning about Hamilton Homes. It wasn't all good news, not by any means. She tried to read the set of his mouth, the angle of his body, but it was hopeless. She didn't know him well enough. She found herself distracted by the play of winter's odd blue-hued sunlight against the black of his hair.

"You wouldn't know it now," Roc said, breaking into her abstraction with a plaintive voice, "but twenty years ago I was a great deal more handsome than our Danny Boy. I was a big man, a man's man, not puny like this fellow here."

"I'm six-two, you old liar," Daniel said without taking his eyes from the documents.

Roc chortled. "Puny, like I said." He stretched out, black jeans covering limbs as long and thick as tree trunks. "Me, I'm not an inch under six-five, and if I'd met you twenty years ago I'd have swept you off your feet, Miss Lindsay."

Daniel made one last note on the papers, and, sighing, he let the pen drop to the desk. "Don't you have some caretaking to do, Roc? Big man's man like you? Wood to chop? Roofs to shingle? Dishes to wash?"

"Nothing wrong with a man washing dishes," Roc said defensively, lumbering to his feet. "Still, I'd better go," he whispered to Lindsay as he gathered the empty bowls and munched the last of the grapes. "Danny here can't stand the competition."

When he was gone, Lindsay took a deep breath and, folding her hands in her lap, faced Daniel with the stoic air of a witness taking the stand. For Robert's sake, she had to pull this off. Dear, gentle, improvident Robert, lying in a hospital room right now, impotently worrying, wondering how her interview was progressing.

She waited for the first question, the first scathing comment about what a financial mess Hamilton Homes was in. But the thick silence lengthened uncomfortably. Daniel merely sat with his elbows on his desk, looking contemplatively at her over his steepled fingers, until she felt such tension in her chest that she thought she might scream.

"I know the figures look bad," she said, unable to bear the loaded silence another minute. "Robert's been having some problems lately."

"Evidently," he murmured, his lips against his fingertips.

"Well, don't you have any questions?" She had come armed with facts and proposals, with explanations for Robert's errors and suggestions for how to redeem them. She'd certainly never pictured the interview going like this, with Daniel McKinley sitting there, bored or sleepy or just plain indifferent, his blue eyes half closed, his syllables short and ironic. "Don't you want to know exactly how this happened, what went wrong?"

He smiled behind his fingers, but Lindsay wasn't sure it was a pleasant smile. "I know what happened." When she raised her brows skeptically, his smile broadened and he leaned back in his chair. "Actually, I knew before I even opened these documents—what I've read here has merely confirmed what I already suspected."

"Oh, really?" His tone, so full of a natural, unassumed arrogance, annoyed her. She tightened her hands in her lap. "Why don't *you* tell *me*, then?"

"All right." He laced his fingers behind his head, a posture that made his shoulders seem even more impossibly broad. "I'd say it boils down to the three main problems. First, Robert Hamilton hired too many people, paid them too much, with luxurious benefits, and he could never bring himself to trim away any of the dead wood or lay off unnecessary positions, even during the recession. Your payroll is hopelessly bloated for a company in these financial straits."

Her cheeks stung. She had been telling Robert things just like that for years. "Well, being too generous is hardly a sin, is it?"

He ignored her comment, putting one ankle over his knee to get more comfortable. She noticed that his legs were almost as long as Roc's, though they were lean and muscular beneath the fine wool of his trousers, and didn't resemble tree trunks by any stretch of the imagination.

"Second—he's been building houses in all the wrong places, trying to provide single family homes in areas where the income ratios make apartment living far more logical. Then, in order to sell the places, he's had to make extremely questionable loans. Now there's a huge percentage of defaults which he's refusing to call in. Instead of turning over these houses, trying to salvage his investment, he's carrying these people for months at a time."

She bit her lip. It was true. But it was part of Robert's incredible goodness that he couldn't bring himself to turn a desperate family out onto the streets. Though she had been warning him for months that he couldn't be the Great Provider for long if he let his own company go under, now that Daniel McKinley was criticizing him in that dry, disinterested voice, she suddenly felt absurdly defensive.

"He realizes he's been far too lenient, Mr. McKinley," she said, ready with her prepared speech, though suddenly she felt little hope that she could make this ruthless businessman appreciate how Robert Hamilton's idealism worked. "But, you see, he built his development in response to what he saw as a dire need for adequate housing among these plant workers. It was a tremendous success at first. Frankly, if there hadn't been layoffs, the idea might well have worked."

She took a deep breath. "I wish you could see the subdivision now, Mr. McKinley. These people aren't deadbeats. They've planted trees and gardens. They've started their children in schools. Believe me, they will pay as soon as they can, and you know that this economic downturn won't last forever. Robert was willing to dig into his own pockets, hoping against hope that he could find a way to let these people keep their homes until the economy improved."

"Yes, Robert is a prince among men, I'm sure," Daniel interjected dryly. "But now what? Now we come to the third and perhaps most troubling problem in this misguided troika—he's taken out high-interest loans to cover his debts, and he's secured those new loans with the few good properties he still owns. If he defaults, he'll lose every profitable asset Hamilton Homes possesses, and the company will consist of a couple of hundred families who are busily planting marigolds in yards they can't pay for."

He leaned forward and tapped the thick pile of documents. "And then, Miss Blaisdell, Robert Hamilton won't be able to sell this company for enough cash to buy a pair of gardening gloves."

Lindsay opened her lips to contradict him, but somehow no words would come. Again an uncomfortable silence blanketed the room. While she searched for the perfect answer, she touched her hair, tucking it behind her ear, wishing she had brushed it after that harrowing helicopter ride. She must look completely mussed and flustered. Which, of course, she was. Where had all her carefully crafted speeches disappeared to? Daniel hadn't said anything that Lindsay herself hadn't told Robert a thousand times. Why did hearing it from this man give the criticism so much authority, so much power to crush Robert's good intentions to dust?

"There is one thing I do want to ask you, though," Daniel said suddenly, and though his eyes were still narrowed, they no longer looked bored. They looked focused, probing.

"What is it?" She lifted her chin, ready.

"Why are you here?" He raised a hand to hold off her murmur of surprise. "I mean *really* why are you here? You must have known that the odds of persuading me to buy this business were about a million to one. And I suspect that you would rather jump naked into a river of hungry crocodiles than come begging for special favors from *me*."

For a minute she stared at him, irritated by his confident assurance that she hated being here, that she was still afraid of him. He raised one brow and waited.

"Perhaps you're right," she finally said with all the equanimity she could muster. She had known he'd find a way to bring up the past, and she was ready for it. "But crocodiles, however hungry, rarely have enough liquid capital to pull off a deal like this."

"I see." He almost smiled. He leaned back again slowly. "Right. But you're very young, attractive, capable. Why not go get yourself another job and leave Robert Hamilton to suffer the fate of all misguided martyrs?"

What a question! She stiffened, her short-lived poise evaporating. "Hamilton Homes is special to me, Mr. McKinley. Robert Hamilton is special to me. He's been my employer for three years. He hired me when I was unexpectedly... out of work."

She paused a moment to let the significance of that comment sink in, and then she went on. "He hired me without any references, and he allowed me the flexibility I needed to keep my family together. I owe him a lot for all that. And I intend to help him in any way I can.''

''So that's all there is behind this impassioned defense? Gratitude?'' He tilted his head speculatively. ''I wonder. Could he, perhaps, be more than your employer?''

She narrowed her eyes. ''I'm not sure what you mean.''

''Are you lovers?'' He said the word so offhandedly she could hardly believe she had heard him correctly.

''Lovers?'' A fire rose in her cheeks. ''Of course not!''

She was outraged by the question, and yet her blush was all the more intense because, in a way, Daniel had stumbled closer to the truth than he imagined. Strange as it sounded, she had accepted this desperate mission in part because Robert Hamilton was *not* her lover. He desperately wanted that title...and more. It was his dream, he had hinted, to be her husband someday. It was because that dream would never come true that she felt obligated to make it up to him somehow.

''No,'' she repeated more quietly, trying to quell the stupid blush. ''We're not lovers.'' Not that it was any of Daniel McKinley's business.

Daniel's mouth twisted in an ironic smile. ''You know, I'm almost tempted to believe you. You're much too young to have a lover if the mere word makes you blush.''

''*Tempted* to believe me?'' She rose to her feet, finally too furious to play this stupid game of insinuation and veiled hostility. ''My private life has no bearing on these negotiations, Mr. McKinley, but, just for the record, if I'm blushing it's anger you see on my cheeks, not embarrassed innocence. I'm not accustomed to having my word doubted, and frankly I don't appreciate your condescending attitude toward Robert, who has been a very good friend to me, and to a lot of people.''

His lips thinned. "Perhaps if he had spent less time on friendship and more time on his business—"

But that was too much. She broke in heedlessly, her voice cold and contemptuous, finding with fatal certainty the phrase she'd uttered three years ago.

"Not every employer is a money-mad workaholic with no time for personal relationships, Mr. McKinley."

The instant the words were out, she knew she had crossed some invisible line. She saw him draw his head back slightly, a fighter reacting to a surprise jab. So he remembered, too, she thought—remembered the exact words she had used that day, though he obviously hadn't expected her to use them again.

Deep beneath her anger, she felt a dull pang of regret for having wrenched open their mutual wound. "More importantly, though," she said, talking fast, as if hurrying to bury the insult, "you should learn that not every employee is a rat ready to leap overboard at the first sign of trouble."

The air in the room had gone cold, as surely as if someone had opened a window to the storm outdoors. Daniel was still, frozen except for a subtle whitening around his lips. Her throat felt very dry again, and her heart was suddenly like a stone in her chest. She had, she knew, just put paid to all of Robert's hopes.

"Perhaps not," Daniel said quietly, lethally. "But I'm quite sure that, if you think back on my experience as your employer, Miss Blaisdell, you'll understand why I might have...shall we say...underestimated your passion for loyalty?"

It was an emotional bull's-eye and she felt the shaft of his insult pierce straight through her. Somehow managing not to wince, she bent over his desk and, with fingers that were visibly shaking, began to gather up Robert's papers.

"Yes, of course, I understand perfectly," she said, glad that the trembling in her fingers had not penetrated her voice. "If you'll just please send for another helicopter... I'm sure there must be one somewhere for hire... Robert will pay the fare, whatever it is... and I'll not bother you any further—"

"Damn it." Daniel put out his hand, staying hers by encircling her wrist with his thumb and fingers. "Lindsay—"

But he never got to finish his sentence. Suddenly Roc was there beside them again, the black of his clothes and the gleam of his hook as startling as ever.

"Excuse me, ladies and gentlemen," Roc said, clearing his throat loudly, "but I just wanted to report that I'm off to make up the bed in the guest room."

Daniel's hand tightened on her wrist. Both of them stared, uncomprehending, at the big man. Lindsay saw that his huge arms were full of pale green linens and creamy white blankets.

"The guest room?" The words were Daniel's, but they were echoing hollowly in Lindsay's mind, too. "The guest room? Why?"

"Look out the window, Danny Boy. While you've had your nose stuck in those papers, that storm's been huffing and puffing and trying to blow your house down."

Like a dazed child, Lindsay turned toward the picture window. Even the trees seemed to have disappeared behind a curtain of white. Not just snow. A blizzard. *Oh, my God*, she thought. *A blizzard.*

Daniel hadn't bothered to look. His gaze was steady on Roc, though his hand still manacled Lindsay's wrist. "No flying?"

"Not unless you want your helicopter to end up a Christmas ornament on the nearest Douglas fir."

"How long?" Daniel's words were tight, economical, grim.

"They're saying twenty-four hours," Roc reported, rolling his eyes skeptically. "But what do those windbags ever know about it? Could be an hour or a month."

Daniel turned slowly toward Lindsay, his gaze dropping to their locked hands. He stared in silence a moment, and then a mirthless smile twisted his full lips.

"Well, how about that?" he said, but he didn't seem to be talking to her. He shook her wrist slightly, and the movement made the papers slide helplessly out of her numb grasp. As the white sheets spilled over the desk, onto the floor, he looked up. Finally their eyes met.

"Perhaps we'd better progress to first names, Miss Blaisdell. It looks as if we're going to be roommates."

CHAPTER TWO

DANIEL paced in front of the picture window, trying not to listen as Lindsay talked to Christy on the telephone. The younger girl was obviously all broken up to hear that Lindsay wasn't coming home. From what he could hear of the one-way conversation, Daniel deduced that she dreaded the thought of spending the night with her grandparents and was putting up quite a fuss.

"Christy, honey, I'm sorry, but you're just too young to stay alone all night," Lindsay was saying again. She'd been like a record stuck on that sentence for the past five minutes. Daniel marveled at her patience even while he longed to snatch the telephone out of her hand and tell that spoiled kid to shut up, for God's sake. There were worse things than an impromptu sleep-over at grandma's house.

But then he hadn't ever been very good with kids. Even his own.

Especially his own.

So he refrained from suggesting that a firmer hand might cut down some of the wrangling. Who was he to criticize? And besides, Lindsay looked so wrung out from the battle of wills already. Make that *battles,* plural— the one with her sister *and* the one with him. She looked whipped. She clearly wasn't a born scrapper, was she?

In fact, now that he'd had time to observe her more closely, he began to feel slightly ashamed of the tone he'd taken with her over the Hamilton Homes deal. Was he just so accustomed to playing hardball professionally that he didn't know when to ease up?

Or was it worse than that? Was it perhaps petty and vindictive... and personal? Was it maybe that he hadn't been able to resist retaliating for what she had said about him all those years ago?

Looking at her now, with the haze of swirling snow behind her, he could almost see it all happening again.

"McKinley's wife is missing? Well, I'm not surprised—she probably ran away from *him*," Lindsay had blurted angrily to one of the other stenographers that day, clearly unaware that Daniel was standing in the doorway behind her. "Who wouldn't? Daniel McKinley thinks he's wonderful, but he's just a money-mad workaholic."

In all fairness, Lindsay couldn't have known the truth. Daniel wouldn't discover the truth himself for two whole nightmarish days. The roaring void of grief and pain that had opened at his feet had not yet sucked him down into its final black hopelessness. But, maddened by his fear, he had been looking for someone to lash out at, and Lindsay was elected.

"You, there." His voice had sounded vicious, weird and steely, a half-human, robot voice. "What is your name?"

Everyone in the room had gasped, he remembered. At first Lindsay didn't answer. Her small, oval face had blanched to a sickening, bloodless white, and her eyes had registered mute horror. "Lindsay Blaisdell," she had whispered finally.

"Well, you have five minutes to clean out your desk, Miss Blaisdell," he had ordered in that same alien voice. She was afraid of that voice, he could see that. He was a little afraid of it himself. "You're fired."

He passed his hand over his eyes, as if to wipe away the vision. He didn't want to relive that day. Not now, not ever again. Recalling himself with an effort to the present, he swiveled and paced to the window on the other side of the fire. A safe distance—from there the crackle of the logs muffled Lindsay's words into unintelligible coos and murmurs. He dropped onto the sofa and watched her.

Lindsay Blaisdell. It was ironic, wasn't it? Of all the people with whom he could have been snowbound...

He still hadn't quite recovered from the shock of seeing her climb out of that helicopter. At first he'd thought she hadn't changed a bit. With her long, dark, braided hair wet and tousled from the snow, her cheeks a bright, wind-stung pink, she had looked very much like the naive woman-child she'd been back then.

But fifteen minutes in her company had changed that impression for good. He took a sip of the coffee Roc had left on the end table and tried to analyze where exactly the change had come from.

It wasn't her face. She still had the face of a teenage Madonna, her dark blue eyes set wide apart and tranquil, her mouth full, upturned, serene, her expression one of unassailable innocence.

No, the difference was in her body, he decided. Seen like this, with her back to him, the honeyed firelight trickling along her hip and thigh, which were outlined by her skirt as she leaned against the desk, she looked sexy as hell. Her hips, in particular, were a work of art. Erotic art, straight out of a bad boy's dreams. And a grown man's palms would cup perfectly around them, just where the swell began to flare out from her narrow waist.

Which brought him to Robert Hamilton. Or did it? Daniel gripped his coffee mug tightly, letting the heat burn into his palm. Though her shocked denial had rung true, still...something, *somebody* had to account for the way that body moved. Its sensuality was definitely awakened.

"Christy, honey, I'd better go now. This is long distance, and I'm using Mr. McKinley's telephone."

Lindsay looked at him over her shoulder, her face sheepishly apologetic, and instantly his emotional kaleidoscope refocused, innocence again dominating the picture. With her lower lip between her teeth and her brows knitted in the middle, she looked like a child herself, a nervous kid who was worried that she might have irritated the grown-ups.

He waved her concern away with an upturned hand, suddenly annoyed with himself. He took another swig of coffee, burning his throat with an ill-advised gulp. Oh, hell, what did it matter anyway? Maybe she was as pure as those snowflakes out there. Or maybe she and Hamilton were sleeping together twice a day, as regular as flossing. He, for one, didn't give a damn.

"I'm sorry that took so long," she said suddenly, and he looked up to see that she had cradled the receiver. Sighing, she rubbed the back of her neck with one hand. "I think this must be the onset of adolescence. She argues with me about absolutely everything."

"Yes, I hear the teenage years can be fairly hairraising," he said politely. "I assume Christy doesn't consider going to her grandparents' house exactly a trip to Disneyland."

"Oh, I don't know," Lindsay said, still kneading her neck. "Come to think of it, the old place does bear a slight resemblance to the Haunted Mansion." She walked over to stand near him by the fire, her upraised hand resting behind her head, her loosened braid spilling in thick, dark waves over her arm. "But you're right, of course. Christy doesn't feel comfortable with her grandmother. Even before our parents died, we were never—'' she seemed to be looking for the right word ''—very close.''

"Well, maybe we'll get lucky, and the storm will pass through quickly," he said. He hoped it would, and not just for her sake. For three years now he had spent the winters up here alone. The snowbound days were the best. Cut off from work, friends, television, telephone and sometimes even Roc, he could sink numbly into the brooding silence. It felt right, this frozen prison. It was the only time he didn't have to pretend to anyone, and he wouldn't welcome having Lindsay Blaisdell as a cellmate. "You may be able to get home before she's out of school tomorrow."

"Oh, good heavens, yes! I *have* to get home by tomorrow," she exclaimed, wide-eyed, as if she hadn't considered the possibility that this could go on longer than twenty-four hours. "It's only four days till Christmas!" She added the last as if that fact alone decided the matter.

He hesitated, hardly able to credit the ingenuous faith he heard in her voice. Apparently she still believed that Fate intervened to protect the dreams of the innocent. Usually such naiveté made him impatient—he had made a religion of facing difficult truths, and he insisted that those around him do the same.

Natural disasters didn't pause for Christmas dinner. The storm front might stall right over them, trapping them here for days, only to be followed by treacherous winds, buried roads, ice storms, downed trees and power lines, a hundred dangers that would make escape impossible. She might be smarter to plan on celebrating New Year's Eve with her little Christy.

Those were the facts, whether she liked them or not. But, strangely, the words wouldn't come. He found himself curiously reluctant to burst that bubble of guileless innocence. It was really a rather pretty thing, though useless, of course...and doomed, too, like an exquisite ice sculpture sparkling under a noonday sun.

And so he didn't speak. A moment of silence stretched into two, then three, as she toyed abstractedly with her braid and he sipped at his coffee.

In a moment she sighed and, letting go of her hair, seemed to straighten herself and return to business.

"If you don't mind, I'll need to telephone Robert, too," she said, her manner crisp, as if she regretted her lapse into such a personal discussion. "He'll be wondering when I'm coming back. I'll be glad to charge it to his calling card—"

Daniel shifted against the cushions. Obviously she was uncomfortable with being obliged to accept the hospitality of a man she disliked. He understood the reluctance to put herself in his debt, but this was absurd. What would be next—offering to pay for her meals? "Don't be ridiculous," he said. "Call direct. I'm quite sure my company won't go bankrupt over a few extra long-distance bills."

She smiled coolly. "Sorry. It's just that over at Hamilton Homes, you see, we worry a lot about things like that."

"Yes," he agreed, glancing at the stack of documents. "I suppose you do." But she was still smiling, and he realized that her comment had been mildly sarcastic. So—she wasn't quite as naive as all that, was she?

She drew a deep breath. "Mr. McKinley—"

"Daniel," he corrected. "We're living together, remember?"

"Yes...Daniel." But she swallowed the last syllable, and he knew she felt funny saying the name. Well, that was only natural, he supposed. If she still worked for him, he would never have invited her to use his first name. And he suddenly wondered whether, if he made the clearly mad move of buying Hamilton Homes, she would be his employee once again.

"When I call Robert," she was saying, "he's going to want to know where the negotiations stand. I know you said there was only one chance in a million that you would ever accept this deal—"

"Right."

She met his gaze directly, though a certain rigidity in her posture made him wonder if she were as tranquil as she'd like him to believe.

"Is that still your position?" She took a deep breath. "You've seen the papers now. Has anything in those documents changed your mind?" Her gaze finally flickered. "Or anything in our discussion?"

He shrugged his shoulders. "As I told you—I haven't learned anything from those papers that I didn't know before," he said. "And I haven't heard you say anything I hadn't heard you say before, either, have I?"

She shook her head slightly. "I suppose not."

"So, no. Nothing has changed. The odds were one in a million before you got here, and they remain one in a million now."

"Are you sure?" She turned her deep, wide gaze on his face, her eyes studying his searchingly. "You see, Robert really can't afford to cherish hopes that are worthless. If there isn't even that one remote chance in a million, we'll need to pursue other options."

"Other options?" He let his skepticism seep into the words.

She flushed, but her voice was firm. "Yes. So I hope you'll be honest, and you won't hold out false hope just so that things won't be so awkward while we're stuck here together."

"Awkward?" Putting his coffee mug back on the end table, he stood up. The motion brought him within a foot of where she stood, and he could smell the sweet floral scent of her perfume, which had been released by the warmth of the fire. He felt a sudden flare of irritation toward Robert Hamilton for letting her venture out into the corporate jungle to do his dirty work for him.

"I'm not afraid of 'awkward', Lindsay," Daniel said bluntly. "In fact, where business is concerned, I thrive on it." He gestured toward the telephone. "So go on— call Robert and tell him the fates have given him a reprieve. It's a million to one right now, but you've got until this blizzard passes to improve the odds."

Half an hour later, Lindsay followed the rhythmic sounds of a pounding ax until she came to the source of the noises, a small woodshed just outside the kitchen door. Assuming that she would find Roc splitting logs, she eased open the door just a few inches and poked her head out.

To her surprise, though, it was Daniel, not Roc, and immediately all other thoughts slipped out of her mind like rain down a windowpane. No longer in the suit and tie he'd been wearing when she first saw him, he now wore jeans and a blue-striped shirt, the sleeves of which had been rolled up above his elbows to allow a greater range of motion.

He didn't seem to notice the cracked door. His attention was focused on the large, squat cylindrical log that stood on some sort of pedestal in front of him. His legs were planted with a squared-off determination, and his bare arms were raised high and to one side. They seemed to hold just a second, and then, with a sudden, violent grace, they swept down, burying the head of the ax several inches deep into the log. Bracing one boot-clad foot on the pedestal, he worked the ax free and then set up a new log and prepared to strike again.

And again, and again. Lindsay was mesmerized, watching as those powerful arms swung up and down, the head of the ax winking in and out of the pale light that filtered through the cracks in the boarded walls of the shed.

It was obviously strenuous work. Though his breath condensed in the frigid air, and snowflakes blown in through the open door dusted the curls on his head, still Daniel was damp from his exertions. Sweat beaded along the gold-ribboned muscles of his forearms and ran in rivulets along the column of his throat. Lindsay shivered, her senses confused by the startling discordance of moist heat against this chilling cold.

Shutting her eyes, she gripped the doorknob, awash with a sense of her own inadequacy. She was a city girl, a Southerner by birth who had never spent a winter north of Phoenix, where she and Christy now lived. She found it disturbing in some primitive way, this display of brute force aligned against nature. And somehow humbling. Never before had she appreciated what was required to create the firewood that crackled so merrily in her Christmas hearth. Now she saw that each log must be wrenched, unwilling, from the massive forest that covered this mountainside.

"How's Robert?"

She opened her eyes, and when her focus returned she saw that Daniel had set down his ax and was standing, his foot propped on the pedestal and his arms folded over his knee, looking at her. Though he still gleamed with sweat, he wasn't even breathing heavily. He was, she thought, no stranger to hard work in spite of his immaculately groomed business persona.

"He's okay," she said. "Still groggy, though. They're giving him a lot of pain pills, I think."

Daniel wiped his brow, then raked his fingers through his hair. When he brought his hand down, his fingertips were damp with melted snow. "Did you tell him about the blizzard?"

She nodded, reluctant to discuss that part of her conversation. Robert had been horrified to hear that Lindsay was trapped on the mountain with Daniel McKinley. He had berated himself so unmercifully for putting her in that predicament that Lindsay had been almost unable to calm him down. Only her promise that she'd be extremely careful had helped at all. So promise she had, though she wasn't sure exactly what Robert wanted her to be careful *of*.

Could he have been jealous, worried that she might find herself attracted to Daniel? Well, if that was it, Robert had nothing to worry about. She hadn't ever been interested in domineering, macho types. And Daniel McKinley looked just as arrogant here, splitting logs in his shirtsleeves, as he ever had in his business suit. She looked at the logs that had fallen so easily under his ax, and she swallowed hard. Maybe more so.

"That looks exhausting," she said, hoping to change the subject before he asked more about her conversation with Robert. "Can I help?"

He raised his brows, obviously surprised. "Thanks, but it's under control," he said. "We were already stocked up, but I thought we'd better have some extra logs lying around in case we lose electricity. Heating three bedrooms will really eat up the wood."

Three bedrooms. She was the problem, then, the reason that he was laboring out here in the bitter cold. "I'm sorry to be an extra burden—" she began, but he broke in impatiently.

"You're not to blame for the blizzard." He picked up the ax and drove it into the pedestal, as if that were its natural storage spot. "You're just as much a victim of the weather as we are."

"I know, but..." But what? She didn't know what to say. She couldn't say what was really on her mind, that she couldn't imagine how she was going to get through the next twenty-four hours. All this idle time cooped up with a man with whom the only thing she had in common was a short, disastrous past acquaintance and a mutual distrust. All this artificial intimacy with this intensely male autocrat who didn't even like her.

She wished Roc would come back from making up the guest room. Or, better yet, she wished she had something to *do*. Yes, that was the answer. She needed to contribute somehow so that she wouldn't feel so helpless and dependent.

"How about if I make some dinner?" She cast a quick glance behind her into the large, intelligently arranged kitchen, and her mood lightened at the thought of puttering about in here. It had been ages since she'd had such a luxurious setting—and so much free time—in which to indulge her favorite hobby. The kitchen in her apartment at home was neat and clean, but tiny. And she was always in a flurry, bolting in the door after work and trying to throw something simple together while helping Christy with her algebra.

She turned back to Daniel, but to her dismay he was shaking his head. "Roc will do it," he said, casually dashing her hopes while he rolled his sleeves down and buttoned them around his wrists. "He's stocked the pantry for the winter, and he has menus lined up from now until Easter. Believe me, there's no need for you to worry about the food."

"But I love to cook," she said, stepping back to allow Daniel to enter the kitchen. His sleeve brushed her hand as he passed by, and the cotton was cold and damp, raising goose bumps up the length of her forearm. She backed away further. "Maybe Roc would let me help him, at least."

Daniel bent over the kitchen sink, splashing water on his face, then rubbed it with the nearest kitchen towel. "No," he said again. "There's no need for you to worry. Roc should have your room ready by now. Would you like to go upstairs, maybe have a shower and a nap? We usually have dinner about seven, if that suits you. Roc could call you then."

"A nap?" She couldn't believe her ears. "It's only three o'clock in the afternoon, Mr. McKinley—I mean, Daniel." She smiled, just a little, to soften the intensity of her instinctive outburst. "I haven't had a nap in the afternoon since I was in kindergarten."

He looked slightly displeased, and she suddenly wondered uncomfortably whether he'd been trying to get rid of her. Maybe she was being rude—maybe snowbound etiquette demanded that she withdraw obediently to her assigned quarters and at least pretend to sleep for the next four hours.

"There must be things you'd like to do." His impersonal gaze roamed over her hair, her face, her hands, and she flushed, thinking what a mess she must look. He probably was accustomed to women who were far more concerned with their grooming than they were with cooking dinner. She lifted her chin, meeting his critical survey with just a touch of defiance. She wasn't an ornamental, trophy female. She was a working woman, and she wasn't a bit ashamed of it. Still, she tucked her short, unpolished nails behind her back.

"You're not an employee here, you know," he said curtly. "You're a guest."

Yes, she thought, but an unwanted guest. A guest who had been invited only by the storm. But she didn't say it, knowing it would sound ungrateful. And she was grateful, of course. Though she would have preferred to be stranded almost anywhere else on earth, she knew how lucky she was not to be out there in that helicopter with that crazy pilot at the controls.

"Still," she said, "there must be things to do during an emergency like this. I'd like to help."

"For God's sake, say yes, man, before the lady decides you're some kind of chauvinist pig." Roc appeared in the doorway, and Lindsay, though grateful for his arrival, wondered whether the caretaker knew a labyrinth of secret passages that accounted for these dramatic manifestations.

He ambled into the kitchen, his black garb strikingly dark against the gleaming white tile. "Daniel really isn't a chauvinist, Miss Lindsay, though I know he's been talking like a chowderhead. He hires plenty of women at the office, even has a couple of female vice presidents, believe it or not."

Lindsay thought back and remembered that this was true, though she wasn't sure why Roc was bringing it up now.

"It's just that he's not accustomed to having useful women right here in the house with him," Roc went on. "Jocelyn, for instance—"

Daniel's hand moved. "Roc—"

"Jocelyn, for instance," Roc continued as if there had been no interruption, "could easily have spent four hours tending those talons of hers. Coloring them some Day-Glo red that would make a blind man wince. And then she would have wanted Danny Boy here to spoon feed her while the paint dried." Roc shuddered, as if the memory were too horrible to bear. "Disgusting."

"That's enough, Roc," Daniel said, and though he still leaned up against the counter, apparently relaxed and at ease, his knuckles were pale around the dish towel he held, and every syllable was as sharp as glass. "I don't think Lindsay's interested in all that."

Of course she *was* interested, though she tried to keep her face bland, noncommittal. What an incredible image Roc had conjured up! She looked at Daniel now, trying to imagine this scowling man sitting on the edge of his wife's bed, laughingly placing bits of fruit between lovely red lips.

"Well, excuse me for trying to defend your sorry reputation," Roc said huffily. He stomped over to the pantry and, grabbing the cupboard handle with his hook, flung it open. "If you want Miss Lindsay to believe that in your opinion women spend all day snoozing and scarfing bonbons, it's no skin off my nose. But I for one would be glad of a little help around here. God knows *you're* worthless."

Lindsay instinctively held her breath, waiting for Daniel's reaction. If she remembered correctly from her days as his employee, cold, quick annihilation awaited the disrespectful caretaker. But when she glanced over at Daniel, she saw that a grudging smile had begun to tilt the corners of his eyes. Roc wasn't just an ordinary employee, then, was he? He obviously had a special status and was allowed liberties that no one else would have dared to take.

The smile disappeared as quickly as it came. Daniel tossed the towel onto the counter.

"All right, Lindsay," he said, his voice betraying neither enthusiasm nor annoyance. "If you want to cook dinner for us tonight, Roc obviously will welcome you into his kitchen. I'm going out to check the furnace."

"Right," Roc said, his head still buried in the pantry. "Then *you* can go take a shower and a nap, Danny Boy. If anyone in this kitchen needs to tend to his grooming, it's you. You smell like the woodpile, boss, and that's a fact."

Daniel deliberately postponed his shower for several hours, concentrating on first one chore and then another, as if to prove to Roc that he didn't mind being grubby and disheveled around Lindsay Blaisdell. Then, when he finally did clean up, he consciously decided to dress down—fresh jeans and a thick blue sweater would be fine. Roc had better understand right now that Daniel wasn't interested in impressing Lindsay Blaisdell.

He had been the victim of Roc's matchmaking for three years now, and he knew all the signs. Ever since Jocelyn had died, the caretaker had been indefatigable in his hunt for some sweet young thing to bring home to Daniel.

The younger and sweeter, the better, at least in Roc's estimation. Apparently he believed that Daniel needed the perfect sugarplum princess as an antidote to Jocelyn, who had been six years older than he, and had been possessed of a sophistication as sharp as the business end of a razor blade.

At first he'd been too numb to notice. But when he'd finally caught on to Roc's machinations, Daniel had been rather sharp himself. He had no intention of ever falling in love again, he had assured his caretaker, and the few ultra-temporary, mutually satisfying relationships he *was* interested in couldn't be honorably offered to these in-genues. These young women were dreaming of fourteen-carat, ring-finger, bells-and-preachers, capital-L-Love, and Daniel was permanently out of the stuff.

But for months Roc had been irrepressible, until finally, in an icy fury, Daniel had found the words to put a stop to the charade.

"Frankly, Roc, I don't believe I require the services of a pimp," he had said, narrow-eyed and steely. Roc had, for once, been speechless. In high dudgeon he had stormed off, but he had, to Daniel's immense relief, finally ceased his maneuvers.

And now, after a blessedly quiet year, apparently Fate had dropped Lindsay Blaisdell like a bomb into the middle of Roc's best intentions. She met all the criteria. Young—Daniel figured somewhere around twenty-two or -three. Pretty—well, even cold-hearted men who had no interest in capital-L-Love still had eyes in their heads, didn't they? And as for sweet—well, Roc was clearly already prepared to plop the Miss Sugarplum Princess tiara on Lindsay's soft dark hair.

The only real problem was that, for the first time, Daniel found himself drawn to the dulcet confection with which Roc was preparing to tempt him. Lindsay's sweetness wasn't like that of the others. Those women would have bored him silly in three days flat, their incessant, unrelieved goodness acting like a sickening surfeit of cotton candy. But Lindsay...well, she was a more complicated dish, sweet, but with the suggestion of subtle spices that would please a far more discriminating palate.

But wait... Daniel sat on the edge of the bed, horrified. What insufferable, arrogant nonsense was this?

Disgusted with his own thoughts, he shoved his feet into his loafers with such force that he nearly tore the leather. Who the devil did he think he was, contemplating this perfectly decent young woman as if she were

the latest delicacy served up on his table? Had he begun,
God help him, to think like Roc?

He ran frustrated hands through his hair and then refused to comb it again as a dumb but nonetheless gratifying symbolic gesture of renunciation. He descended
the stairs, his determination renewed. He was not going
to act like the wicked wolf, feasting shamelessly on the
honeyed goodness of little Lindsay Blaisdell while she
was lost in his snowy forest.

Besides, Lindsay Blaisdell was already on to him, and
might not make such easy pickings as all that anyway.
She had decided three years ago that Daniel was a self-
centered bastard, and he was not going to try to change
her mind.

Why should he? She was right.

CHAPTER THREE

DINNER was tense but mercifully uneventful, thanks to Roc, who, as if he sensed Lindsay's discomfort, kept up a colorful monologue about dirty politics in some country she had never heard of. A country, she suspected, that he had invented on the spur of the moment.

When Roc left the table to do the dishes, forbidding Lindsay to follow him, she had a moment of panic, but without skipping a beat Daniel smoothly segued into a discussion of the weather. Gratefully Lindsay followed his lead, and they managed to make the subject last, though by coffee they were practically down to naming individual snowflakes. As soon as civility allowed, Lindsay excused herself, pleading exhaustion, and fled upstairs.

Her room was large, warm and surprisingly welcoming. The pale green linens Roc had put on the bed matched the flowered drapes, honey-gold wood paneling lined the walls and built-in bookcases, and a small fire was already chattering away in the hearth. Someone had thoughtfully laid an oversize white sweatshirt across the bed, and, not even bothering to wonder who it belonged to, she shrugged out of her uncomfortable business suit gratefully and slipped the sweatshirt on. It came down almost to her knees.

The relief was instant and overwhelming. Her defenses down, the stressful day finally overtook her, and she realized that, though it was only seven o'clock, she could hardly keep her eyes open. She slid under the eiderdown comforter and felt her body relax for the first time today. She tried to worry about Christy, or Robert, or the future of Hamilton Homes, but she simply wasn't up to it. Shutting her eyes, she promptly fell into a deep, dreamless sleep.

She should have known she'd have to pay for that craven escape, and the bill came due at 3:00 a.m., when she woke with a start, wondering where she was and why she was so cold.

When she remembered, it didn't make her feel one bit better.

Three o'clock was the most godawful lonesome corner of the night, she decided, sitting up in bed and hugging her pillow against the homesick ache under her breastbone. The fire had burned itself out, one half-charred log still lying among the pile of sickly gray ashes. Her clothes, which she had so carefully draped across the chair last night, looked weirdly empty, as if their owner had vaporized, leaving them behind.

Worst of all, when she stood up and peered out the window, she saw by the illumination of the yard lights that the blizzard had not subsided at all. If anything, it was whiter and angrier than ever, with snow flying in so many directions at once it was impossible to tell which way the wind was blowing. Her heart dragged at her chest as she reluctantly faced the truth: she probably wouldn't be going home today, either. She didn't know how she would face Christy's tears.

She felt a little like crying herself, though weeping was a weakness she despised and rarely indulged in, at least not since her parents had died. Though she had been only twenty years old at the time, that catastrophe had taught her a lot about survival. She had realized then that happiness was a trophy, not a gift—and that weepers rarely carried the trophy home.

But damn, damn, damn, damn! She pressed her hands over the frigid glass, letting the snowflakes beat their silent tattoo against her palms. She lowered her forehead to the window, too, though she shivered as the cold seeped into her skin. She felt so impotent, trapped here in this luxurious prison when Christy needed her.

The room, which had felt spacious last night, seemed to be closing in on her. Her frustration called for motion, even pointless motion. Swiveling, she hurried toward the door, opened it in careful silence, and began to pick her way down the darkened staircase without any particular destination in mind.

Dimmed track lighting along the ceiling spotlighted just enough of the stairway to make her trek safe. She found the kitchen without making a sound, poured a mug of milk and then, just as quietly, headed into the living room.

The outdoor porch was illuminated, and the wide picture windows on either side of the hearth offered a panoramic view of the blizzard. As a result, the room was silver-blue with snowlight, and the shadows of silently writhing trees subtly undulated across the walls. Feeling eerily as if she walked under water, she moved instinctively toward the giant central fireplace, which, even unlit, was somehow both architecturally and emotionally the heart of the house.

She paused abruptly, sensing Daniel even before she saw him. As her eyes adjusted a little to the blue-gray gloom, she made out his form. He sat in the upholstered armchair, turning something around in his hands, staring into the empty fireplace as if he hadn't noticed the flames had gone out hours ago. Something that felt like fear seized her, and her legs tensed, preparing to make an exit unnoticed.

"Lindsay," he said, his voice low. "Come in. Sit down."

Her heart contracted, and her movements faltered. She knew that voice, that middle-of-the-night monotone. Somehow, in spite the haunting sadness of the sound, in spite of the unfamiliarity of her surroundings and the forbidding hour of the night, she wasn't afraid anymore. Her father's voice had sounded that way, night after night, in the months after her mother had died.

She moved further into the room, no longer considering retreat. No matter how she felt about Daniel McKinley in the daytime, she wouldn't leave her worst enemy alone like this. She had learned the hard way that the real danger came when sorrow and solitude spent too much time together. Luckily, she was proficient at being grief's companion.

She only hoped Daniel wasn't drunk. Her father had always kept these midnight vigils with a bottle of Scotch. She eased toward the sofa, trying to see if Daniel, too, held a lonely glass of amber courage.

"Can't you sleep, Lindsay?" She couldn't see much of his face as he spoke, except for his eyes, which shone in the pearly shadows as he watched her come around and sit on the edge of the sofa. "Is it too cold in the house? I can adjust the thermostat if you like."

His words weren't slurred at all, she noticed, though they had a remote indifference that belied the concern implicit in the questions. He asked the right things, but somehow only by rote, as if he were repeating dimly understood foreign sentences from a Berlitz tape. *Excuse me, is this the train to Frankfurt? How much for a ticket, please?*

Setting her milk on the end table, she adjusted the long sweatshirt over her knees and folded her hands in her lap. "No, the temperature's fine. I think I just went to sleep too early."

"Yes," he said, nodding, rolling the object he held between his palms. "That's probably it."

Now that her eyes had adjusted to the strange light, she could just barely make out what he held. Not a drink, she saw with relief, but something smaller. A wooden carving...a chess piece? She tried to see more, but it was hard to distinguish details without conspicuous staring.

"How about you?" she asked. "Can't you sleep, either?"

"I was just about to go upstairs," he said. "I've been working late."

She knew it was a lie, and not just because of the endless hours she had spent watching her father. This room was abnormally still, as if the air currents hadn't been disturbed in hours, and Daniel himself was as immobile as if he were a piece of the furniture, giving off a profound languor that amounted to emotional paralysis. He had been in that chair for hours, and she knew that he hadn't planned to leave, perhaps for hours more. If she had not come down, he probably would, like her father, have watched the dawn rise with empty, red-rimmed eyes.

Except that Daniel hadn't been crying. His eyes, which watched her so unblinkingly, had a cold, dry gleam that was as hard as ice. She shivered suddenly, realizing that this wasn't really like her father's grief, which had been wild but somehow weak. This grief was huge, mute, immobile, and allowed itself no refuge in either tears or an alcoholic anesthesia.

"The snow doesn't seem to be letting up at all, does it?" It was a lame beginning, but she needed to get him talking. It had been easier with her father. She'd known him better, known which subjects she could eventually coax him into discussing safely: Christy's grades, their meddling grandparents, the decline of the American political system. She'd known where the conversational land mines were, too—flowers, music, illness…anything that would remind him of her mother.

With Daniel, though, the territory was uncharted. "Robert is more familiar with winter storms than I am, I guess. He warned me that my chances of going home today weren't very good."

Daniel still didn't answer, so she tried again. "How many inches do you suppose have fallen since the blizzard began? Or would it be feet by now?"

His hands jerked slightly. "I don't know." His voice had harshened. "And I don't care. We've already done the subject of the snow to death tonight, don't you think?"

"Yes, I guess we did." She made herself smile softly, though she felt a little stung by his tone. "Well, what would you like to talk about?"

He stared down at the chess piece in his flat palm, as if he were surprised to find it there. Lindsay looked, too. It was the white queen, a miracle of ivory so intricately carved it looked like lace. Of course, Lindsay thought miserably. The queen.

"I don't," he said slowly, "want to talk at all."

Lindsay's hands tightened in her lap. The flat rejection in his voice was strangely hurtful. She couldn't think why, really. She had been through this so many times with her father. He had always resisted her company, rejected at the beginning any effort to bring him out of his despair, the way a drowning man sometimes clawed and fought against his rescuer. She knew that, no matter how it sounded, it wasn't personal.

But this time it *felt* personal. She looked at Daniel's strong hand as he wrapped it around the fragile figure. "Would you prefer to be alone?"

He nodded. "Yes," he said. "Perhaps that would be better." Then, shutting his eyes, he leaned his head against the back of the chair. It was as if he simply ceased to be in the room. Lindsay had never felt so completely dismissed.

There was no point in delaying. And why should she want to? She stood, smoothing her palms down the soft cotton of the sweatshirt that nearly reached to her knees. She picked up her mug, still full of lukewarm milk, and moved slowly toward the staircase.

Ten steps away, she stopped and turned back to the silent room. Daniel's eyes were open, again glimmering in the mother-of-pearl light as he watched her silently.

"I just want you to know...I wasn't trying to intrude," she said, wondering why she felt defensive. She hadn't done anything wrong. *She* hadn't been rude—she had only tried to help. "You *did* invite me to come in, you know."

"I know," he said, his voice low and weary. "I thought—" But he broke the sentence off, turning his head away. "I'm sorry, Lindsay. It was a mistake."

She came downstairs as late as possible the next morning. Though it was well after eleven by then, the dense gray snow clouds still blocked the sun so completely that the house wore the long shadows of twilight. Not even the brave illumination of every available lamp could completely dispel the unnatural gloaming.

She walked slowly, reluctant to encounter anyone. Actually, she had almost decided to hide in her room all day. She felt like such an interloper here, especially after her sympathetic overtures had been rebuffed so thoroughly last night. Daniel didn't want her around, that was obvious. And though Roc was much more welcoming...well, it wasn't his house, was it?

She had half hoped that, because she had risen so late, Daniel might already have breakfasted and disappeared into work or chores. She was surprised, therefore, to find Daniel and Roc standing side by side in the kitchen, watching reports of the storm on the small television set that angled out from the corner cabinet.

Heavy goosedown jackets hung over the pegs next to the kitchen door, as if the two men had just come in—or were on their way out. She felt self-conscious suddenly in her white sweater and full gray skirt, an utterly useless outfit if ever there was one. But she had nothing else to wear. She had arrived expecting a couple of hours of business negotiations, not a weekend of shoveling snow and splitting logs.

They, on the other hand, were both sensibly dressed in working clothes—well-worn boots, faded jeans and long-sleeved flannel shirts. Roc's outfit was, as usual, entirely black, and he looked rather like a thick, tall stovepipe. But Daniel's old jeans rode every curve, every muscle with an easy intimacy, and his shirt was a muted plaid of blue, black and silver that was ridiculously becoming.

Lindsay forced herself to look around the room. It was the only spot in the house that was really bright, the fluorescent lighting bouncing merrily off the yards of white tile. The smell of coffee brewing was equally reassuring. She ventured in a few more feet.

Roc noticed her first. "Miss Lindsay," he called, sounding gratifyingly thrilled to see her. "Come in, come in! We're trying to finish off the last of the fresh berries. After that, if these yammering TV peacocks know what they're talking about for once, I guess it's going to be canned pork and beans for us for a while."

He pulled out the chair nearest to Daniel and whisked a placemat onto the table. From nowhere appeared a stoneware pitcher of milk, a bowl of cereal, and a dish of mixed berries, clearly just washed and shining delightfully in shades of ebony, garnet and crimson. Lindsay couldn't think of any way to avoid sitting down, so she simply smiled her thanks and did so.

"Good morning, Lindsay." Leaning against the countertop, Daniel watched as Roc opened her napkin with a flourish and draped it over her lap. "Did you ever get to sleep last night?"

"Yes, I did. I slept quite well," she lied, accepting the spoon Roc was handing her. She stared into Daniel's ironic blue gaze. "How about you?"

"Absolutely," he said with a wry smile. "Like a baby."

Okay, she thought, scattering a few berries over the top of her cereal irritably. So they were both lying. Well, it was more civilized than telling each other outright to mind their own business, she supposed. But just barely.

She turned to Roc, who was pouring milk into her bowl, obviously enjoying his role as the most conscientious of waiters. "Is the news really bad this morning?"

"Not if you're a tow truck driver, a flashlight salesman or an undertaker," he said, setting down the pitcher and shrugging over at the television in disgust. "But it sounds like the rest of us dumb chumps are in for a pretty mangy week."

"Week?" Lindsay's spoon faltered halfway to her mouth. "They're not really saying this will go on for a *week*, are they?"

Roc nodded grimly. "But what do they know? Meteorologists!" The way he said it, the word was an insult. "Just a bunch of prissy pants who use too much hair spray! Rots their brains, I tell you, till they wouldn't know a cold front from a rat's backside!''

Lindsay looked forlornly toward the television, where footage of half-buried cars and downed power lines alternated with animated weather maps. A week? It was already the twenty-first. If she were trapped here a week, Christy would have to spend Christmas at their grandparents' town house, which was arguably the coldest, most depressing domicile on this planet.

"Oh, no," she said, recoiling from the idea. "I can't possibly stay here through Christmas."

"Really?" Without moving an inch, still leaning against the countertop with his arms folded across his chest, Daniel tossed a hard glance her way. "You can't? Why not?"

"It's Christy," she explained, surprised by his question. Hadn't she made it clear yesterday that she had important responsibilities at home—that Christy wasn't the kind of child who could be farmed out to relatives? Not after what she'd been through. "She'd be heartbroken."

"Oh, for heaven's sake. Christmas is just a word, you know," Daniel said, his voice curiously tense. "Just postpone the celebration until you do get home and call it Christmas. It won't make a bit of difference to a twelve-year-old as long as she gets all her presents."

"No," she said slowly, lowering her spoon to the bowl, her appetite gone. "You don't understand Christy. She's very sentimental, very fragile. Things like Christmas mean a lot to her." She rubbed at her forehead, wishing she didn't have to try to explain this to a man like Daniel McKinley. He probably worked all day on Christmas, just as he did every other day of his life.

"Oh, what a mess," she murmured, half to herself. "What will I tell her?"

"Why don't you tell her to count her blessings?" Daniel straightened, letting his arms fall to his sides. The motion, combined with his grim tone, was somehow ominous. "Tell her you're safe and warm, with a roof over your head. Tell her to be grateful."

For a minute Lindsay just stirred her cereal, trying to hang on to her temper. But it was an uphill battle, especially when her nerves were already so frayed. He was such an unfeeling man. This superior, domineering tone was almost intolerable.

"Grateful? As *I* should be?" Lindsay straightened her back, too, and though she kept her voice low it carried a distinct chill. "Is that what you're trying to say?"

"Now, Miss Lindsay—" Roc began placatingly.

"No, that's *not* what I'm saying," Daniel broke in. "And you know it." With a harsh motion he flicked off the television and faced Lindsay. "I'm saying there are a hundred thousand people out there who have no heat or running water. A hundred and fifty-seven homes have been destroyed. Eleven people are dead."

His eyes narrowed. "Dead, Lindsay. They won't be celebrating Christmas, not anywhere, not ever. Why don't you tell her that?"

Eleven people already dead! Lindsay's anger faded abruptly, and the last taste of the milk seemed to sour in her throat. She swallowed it down with an effort. Eleven human beings, each with people who had loved and needed them, just as Christy needed her...

She glanced instinctively toward the kitchen window, beyond which she could see only a rather picturesque snowscape, clouded by a torrent of whizzing white flakes. It didn't look like a death trap. Certainly not from in here, where they sat eating fresh berries and watching television.

She felt suddenly ashamed. Daniel was right. This lodge was so well-built, so comfortable and well-stocked, that she hadn't begun to guess how severe the storm really was.

"I'm sorry," she said quietly. "I didn't know."

"Well, Lord Almighty, there's no need for *you* to be sorry, Miss Lindsay." Roc's eyes shot a bullet of intense disapproval toward his boss before he turned back to Lindsay, patting her shoulder consolingly. "Of course you didn't know. As you may have noticed, Danny Boy here has about as much tact as an atom bomb, but I'm quite sure he's just about to realize what an obnoxious lunkhead he's been and apologize to you for being so—"

"All right, Roc. That's enough," Daniel broke in gruffly, raking his hands through his hair and moving toward the breakfast table. "I can do this myself."

He pulled out the chair next to Lindsay's, hoisting one leg over the seat, straddled it backward. Sighing, he rubbed at his dark, tousled hair one more time and looked at her mutely for a moment, as if he didn't know where to begin.

"Roc's right," he said. "I *am* sorry. I was out of line— I shouldn't have lost my temper like that. All I can say in my defense is that I've been watching the news broadcasts all morning, and the stories are harrowing. But that's no excuse, not really. I don't know what your sister's problems are, or what it's like for her at her grandmother's house, so I have no business passing judgment on the situation."

"Well," Lindsay said hesitantly, stunned by his candor. She suspected he didn't apologize easily, or often. "It's just that Christy is—"

"No." Daniel held up his hand. "You don't have to justify anything to me. It's none of my business." He sighed again, heavily, and looked toward Roc, as if for inspiration. "Listen, Lindsay. I know this is difficult for both of us. It's a particularly perverse twist of fate that we should be stranded here together like this, considering how unpleasant our past—"

Roc cleared his throat extravagantly, and Daniel broke off, taking the hint.

"Okay, okay!" Daniel began again. "What I mean is, let's call a truce." He leaned over the chair, his chin on the heel of one hand, and considered her musingly a moment. "What do you say we pretend we've never met each other before? Let's pretend there's no Hamilton Homes deal hanging in the balance. In fact, let's pretend this is just a motel at which we both happen to be staying during the storm, okay?"

He almost smiled, and the blue of his eyes lost some of its icy glitter. "Maybe at the very least we can do away with some of the boss-versus-employee, guest-versus-host, buyer-versus-seller stuff that's been clouding the air around here."

"Way to go, Danny Boy!" Roc chimed in approvingly, slapping the tabletop with his good hand. The berries shivered in their dish, and Lindsay's milk lapped at the sides of her bowl. "Better still, let's pretend *I'm* the innkeeper, and you two are my guests. That way I can keep you both in line."

Daniel flicked a sardonic glance toward the old man. "Well, you can try," he said. Returning his gaze to Lindsay, he raised his brows. "What do you think? Is it a deal?"

"But all this really isn't necessary," she demurred, embarrassed that their mutual antagonism had escalated to the point at which Daniel believed "deals" were required. They were both grown-ups—they should have been able to coexist peacefully whether they liked each other or not. She, particularly, should have been more mature, should have held on to her temper just a little longer. If she hadn't been so worried about Christy, she thought, then surely she could have...

But Daniel was holding out his hand. "Well?" he asked again. She forced her own hand out to meet it. As his fingers closed around hers, her much smaller hand was immediately lost inside the greater power of his. More domination games? she wondered cynically... and then she stopped herself. Hadn't he just offered to relinquish the title of lord and master? "Deal, Lindsay?"

"Of course," she said politely, returning to his forceful grip with all the strength she had, until her ring dug into her palm. Obviously noticing the grimace on her face, he grinned, but she clenched her teeth and didn't let go. "Deal, Daniel."

Later that afternoon, Roc moved a telephone and a small desk into her room, explaining that he realized, even if "some people" didn't, that Lindsay might want a little privacy when she talked to Robert or Christy.

"Especially this Robert guy, right? The one in the hospital?" Roc was bent down, trying to plug the cord into the wall jack, but he looked at Lindsay over his shoulder, as if assessing her response. "Hard to be a very good Florence Nightingale if a bunch of nosey Parkers are breathing down your neck every minute, right?"

She smiled. "Right." It was true—she would be more comfortable talking to Robert alone, though for different reasons. He asked so many questions about Daniel. She was afraid it would be obvious that Robert was suffering from a terrible fit of jealousy. How ridiculous that would seem to Daniel! She could almost picture him now, with that one eyebrow lifted sardonically. Jealous?

And Christy... well, she didn't really want Daniel to hear those conversations, either. Christy wasn't taking Lindsay's absence well, and Daniel could probably hear her whining through the lines.

"So... is this guy like your special guy or what?" Roc was so twisted up, trying to fit his huge frame into the little space between the bed and the end table, that Lindsay could hardly make out his words.

"Who? Robert?"

"Yeah, Robert. I guess that's his name. The guy with the exploding appendix."

She laughed, perching on the edge of the bed, where she could hear him better. "Well, sort of." She sighed, trying to think whether a "yes" or a "no" was more honest. Yes, Robert *wanted* to be her special guy, but no, he wasn't. Not really. "Not as special as he'd like to be, though."

"Good." Roc backed out of the wedge of space, his black-jeaned rump bumping into the table as he wriggled free.

"Why is that good?" She reached out and caught the lamp before it fell. "You don't know Robert, do you?"

"Nah, never met the guy." Roc stood up, his head nearly reaching the low-beamed ceiling as he stretched the kinks out of his back. "But he's not the guy for you. Only a wimp-guts would let their appendix explode on 'em like that."

"Let me guess." Daniel's voice came unexpectedly from the doorway. "Do we have here the indomitable Mr. Richter, superhero extraordinaire, holding forth once more on the frailties of mortal men?"

The older man grunted. "Well, they don't call me Roc for nothing, Danny Boy."

Daniel laughed. "I'm the one who invented that nickname, and I can tell you it had a lot more to do with the impenetrability of your head, actually."

"Well, so what do you want, anyway?" Roc sounded petulant, and he pointedly turned his attention to checking the dial tone on the telephone. "The lady and I were having a private conversation. If you don't mind."

"*She's* more likely to mind than I am," Daniel rejoined. He bent down and picked up a large cardboard box he had brought with him into the hall. "But, if you remember, in your new role as innkeeper you did instruct me to bring this down from the attic. You said to deliver it here pronto." He shoved the box through the doorway. "What in hell is in there, anyway? It weighs a ton."

Roc twinkled a sly grin Lindsay's way, waggling his white eyebrows. "Didn't I tell you? Puny."

Lindsay smiled, but in her heart she couldn't agree. Daniel was much trimmer than Roc, obviously, and maybe a couple of inches shorter, but there was nothing puny about him. Power emanated from every long, lean inch of his six-two frame.

"What's in the box, Roc?" she asked, partly out of curiosity and partly because she could see that Daniel was growing impatient. Why would Roc arrange to put the thing in Lindsay's room? Surely not just for storage. With the new desk, the huge box and both imposing men in here, this large, comfortable room had suddenly seemed to shrink to dollhouse size.

"Clothes," Roc said triumphantly. He pulled out his pocketknife and, popping open the blade by pressing it against his thigh, bent over and ran the cutting edge across the packing tape that held the flaps of the box together. "I have here the result of a brilliant brainstorm—a whole new wardrobe for our lovely visitor."

"What?" Lindsay was mystified. How could Roc have arranged for clothes so quickly? And *how*, when nothing could get either in or out of this lodge? "Clothes for me?"

Daniel was frowning, watching as Roc freed the sides of the box and folded them back. "What clothes, Roc?" He seemed as surprised as Lindsay.

"Use your head, Danny Boy!" Roc clicked his tongue, self-satisfaction evident on his face. "Don't tell me you've forgotten the delicious Doreen?"

Daniel's face lightened, and he threw back his head with a laugh. "Oh, no, Roc—not Doreen!" Something in his tone alerted Lindsay that she might not like what was coming.

"Well, of course Doreen, you dunderhead!" Roc knelt back on his heels and dug around in the box. "Think clearly now. Wasn't she just about Miss Lindsay's size?"

Daniel glanced at Lindsay. "Well," he said slowly, his eyes raking down her body speculatively. "They are about the same height, I guess."

"Right." Roc yanked some turquoise, heavily beaded cloth from the box with his hook and piled it carelessly on the floor. "And about the same weight."

"Think so?" Daniel shook his head, still eyeing Lindsay somberly. "Well, if they are, it's sure distributed differently."

"For God's sake, Danny Boy, just because Lindsay didn't buy her cleavage by the yard from Doc Wonderbody, that's no reason to—"

Lindsay's cheeks pinkened. She reached down and stayed Roc's hand. "Wait a minute, gentlemen," she said. "Who is Doreen?"

"Sorry," Daniel said, his tone politely apologetic. "Doreen was a woman who once visited here for a few days. She was called away unexpectedly and left her things behind. She said she'd send an address, but she didn't ever get around to it.''

It sounded logical, but Lindsay was still skeptical. If that was all there was to it, what was all the laughter about?

From his cross-legged position on the floor, Roc suddenly burst into song. ''Oh, Doreen, Doreen,'' he crooned, holding a preposterous fringed-leather dress up to his massive shoulders, ''you're my hor—''

''Roc!'' Daniel's interruption was sharp.

''Cool your jets, Danny Boy,'' Roc said, scowling. ''This is the family version.'' He cleared his throat. ''As I was saying, Oh, Doreen, Doreen, my *hungry* Cheyenne queen.'' He looked toward Lindsay and winked. ''Hungry for love, that is.''

Lindsay's eyes widened. ''Doreen was a Cheyenne Indian?''

Daniel shook his head, but Roc's laughter doubled. He tickled the fringes on the brown leather dress. ''Thought she was! She was up here looking to take a couple of scalps, too. She really wanted Danny Boy's lovely black locks hanging from her belt, but Jocelyn wasn't about to let any Indian bimbo lay hands on *her* man, was she, Danny?''

The laughter had died out of Daniel's face so quickly Lindsay was startled when she looked over at him. But Roc was absorbed in his perusal of the box, tossing first one strange outfit and then another onto the floor beside him. ''And even Doreen was no match for our Jocelyn. So Doreen settled for that crazy old rich man...Danny, what was his name?''

''Barnes,'' Daniel said, but his voice was as blank as his face, a galaxy away from the lighthearted teasing she'd heard a minute ago. Lindsay's heart twisted. Just the mention of Jocelyn's name was torture to Daniel, wasn't it? Oh, she thought, wishing she could go and touch his stiffened shoulder, he must have loved her very, very much. "The crazy old man's name was Barnes. She married him, as I recall."

Roc had reached the bottom of the box. "Aw, heck, there's nothing down here but beauty aids." He brandished a bottle of pink lotion. "Though, if you ask me, the best beauty aid our Doreen could have is a blind old man for a husband." He looked up. "Right, Danny Boy?"

But Daniel was already gone.

CHAPTER FOUR

ALICE was crying, her sweet voice distorted by low, moaning sobs that would surely break the heart of anyone who listened. It was the saddest noise on earth, yet somehow Daniel wanted to cry with joy at the sound. Alice... It had been so long since he had heard her voice at all. He'd endured so many cold years of silence.

He had to get to her. He struggled against his strangely inert body, but his arms and legs wouldn't answer his mind's frantic commands. *Hurry*, he ordered himself over the rising panic. If he didn't get to her quickly, the crying would stop, and he would be left alone again with the silence. *Run. Fly. Find her.*

Still the mournful sound continued. Daniel moaned, too. Dear God, why couldn't he move? His daughter needed him—she was only six, too little to save herself—it was up to him. But he couldn't move. He couldn't find her. Sweat beaded along his brow, and his arms ached from the need to hold her, to gather her in and keep her safe.

He couldn't get there, not in time. Fear paralyzed him, and in desperation his prayer changed. *Oh, God, please let them find her.*

But they wouldn't. They wouldn't. The moaning became a scream, wrapping itself around the house, around his head...

And then he woke up. For a minute he just lay in the morning-bright room, trying to hear over the noise of his heart, which galloped with painful thuds across his chest. He recognized the moaning sound instantly. It was only the wind, which had intensified dramatically during the night and was whipping past the house like a swarm of keening ghosts.

Only the wind. He pinched the bridge of his nose and took a deep, steadying breath. It was only the wind.

Swinging his feet over the edge of the bed, he sat up, resting his elbows on his thighs and bowing his head as he waited for his heart to slow down. He hadn't dreamed of Alice in a long time, but he knew from past experience that it would take a few minutes to collect himself.

Gradually he began to notice things around him, the brown leather wing-back chair in the corner, the blue throw pillows, the red spine of the book he'd been reading last night. And suddenly he realized that, for the first time in days, the colors in the room were vivid, brightened by strong, natural light.

He glanced over at the window, surprised. Beyond the blue silk frame formed by the drapes, he could see the roof of Roc's cabin clearly. And he could see the trees—many of them pure white two-thirds of the way up, then a deep green at the top, where a prodigious wind had swept them clean of snow. He could even see the subtle jagged line where the silver of nearby mountains met the blue of the sky.

But he didn't see any snow in the air.

The blizzard was over.

As if on cue, the pealing of bells floated up from the great room downstairs. A triumphant Christmas carol was on the stereo—one of his own, long-ignored collection, he suspected. Lindsay or Roc, or both, had unearthed the albums and turned the music on at top volume, as if in celebration. His mouth twisted wryly at his reflection in the mirror across the room. He knew what Lindsay was celebrating, and it wasn't the coming of Santa Claus. It was the departure of the snow. The arrival of her freedom.

He stood up and dressed quickly. He hoped it was true: he hoped, for her sake and for his, that Lindsay Blaisdell would be back in Phoenix before the day was over. On the other hand, this joyous ringing of bells might be premature. The winds were clearly too high for flying—it took a lot of wind to strip the snow from the trees like that. Maybe, just maybe, once the trails were cleared, Roc could get her out of here in the Jeep, as long as the forecast didn't call for more snow. And as long as the Littledale Bridge wasn't iced over—or down altogether.

But all those things were possible, and someone had better warn her before she called her sister with the good news. He shoved his shirttail into his jeans and grabbed a pullover sweater from the drawer. God alone knew what that spoiled kid would do if Lindsay built her hopes up for nothing.

When he got downstairs, his houseguest was already on the telephone. She was half sitting, half reclining on the sofa, her bare feet pulled up beside her. She smiled tentatively as she saw him approach and wiggled her fingers in a small wave, but she didn't stop talking.

"I'm not sure," she was saying. Her voice was light, reflecting the smile. "Roc says it's still too windy to fly, but I'm hoping Daniel will say it's okay to drive. If he does, I could be home by tonight." She paused. "Yes, I know I do. Oh, don't be silly. It's just that, considering we've been stranded up here together, it seemed absurd to keep saying Mr. This and Miss That."

She glanced again in Daniel's direction and, pointing at the receiver, mouthed the word "Robert." He nodded briskly and took the chair behind his desk, where the Hamilton Homes paperwork still lay. What an ass Robert

Hamilton was, he thought, suddenly inexplicably grouchy. This was the twentieth century, wasn't it? Calling a man by his first name was hardly a scandalous intimacy.

"Anyhow..." Lindsay seemed eager to change the subject. "I'll probably be leaving soon anyway. Isn't that great? But still, I don't see how I could get to the hospital until tomorrow at the earliest. I'm so sorry, Robert." She turned her head, so that Daniel could no longer see her face. "I miss you, too."

Tightening his jaw, Daniel scribbled a few notes on his legal pad, pressing down so hard the ballpoint threatened to pierce the paper. For God's sake, did Hamilton have no pride? First he couldn't wait for Lindsay to rush up here to plead his case, and now he couldn't wait for her to come home to hold his hand.

Daniel knew he wasn't being quite fair, of course. Hamilton's medical emergency was obviously genuine— it was pretty hard to fake appendicitis. And Lindsay obviously was eager to do whatever she could to help him. But then, she was a born nurturer. He had heard it when she talked to her sister, and he could hear it now as she coaxed Robert out of his jealous fit, her soothing voice the equivalent of an emotional Band-Aid.

Who took care of Lindsay, he wondered, while Lindsay was busy taking care of those two? Nobody. You could bet the ranch on that.

He forced his attention back to the papers. Luckily, very little in the loan securitization documents had surprised him, and late last night he had received the call from his financial advisor that he had been waiting for. What had been only a rumor was now confirmed: two huge corporate relocations were planned for properties adjacent to the Hamilton Homes development. More jobs and higher property values would inevitably follow.

So finally he was ready to move. His lawyers, toiling through the night, had already generated most of the paperwork. He could fax this memo to his secretary in Phoenix, who was a miracle of efficiency. She could insert the details into the main documents, run them past his lawyer, and then fax the whole thing back to him within a couple of hours. If Lindsay really was able to leave today, she could take the good news instead of flowers to Robert's sickbed.

"Oh, poor Robert, how awful for you!" Lindsay's sympathetic tone was more appropriate for a talk with her twelve-year-old sister than her thirty-year-old boss, and the sound grated hard on Daniel's nerves.

But business had always been his best method of blotting out other irritations, and, thankfully, it was effective now, too. Focusing hard on the notes he was making, he didn't hear another word of Lindsay's conversation. He didn't even hear the Christmas bells, which still rang merrily from the stereo. When he looked up again some minutes later, Lindsay had hung up the telephone and was quietly watching him work.

"Good morning," she said politely. "Did you see?" She gestured toward the window. "No snow!"

He looked out at the strange, undulating white landscape and nodded. It did look peaceful, but he knew the terrain well enough to understand that conditions were still very dangerous. Even shrubs that once had been three feet tall were now completely buried. But, technically, she was right. It was not snowing.

"Yes. That's good news, isn't it?" He tried to sound positive, though even as he spoke the wind tore a plume of snow from one high, crested mound and spun it into the air like a small tornado. Good thing Roc had warned her that the helicopter could never fly in these conditions.

"Oh, yes," she said eagerly. "I'm hoping that, if you can spare Roc to drive me, I'll be able to leave sometime tod—"

"Yes, sometime soon," he broke in before she could say "today." He hated the wistful hope he could hear in her voice, especially when he knew the odds were against an immediate departure. "You haven't called your sister yet, have you?" She shook her head. "Good. There are still plenty of dangers after a storm like this one. I'll have to call the highway patrol, for instance, and see what the roads are like."

"Yes, please, will you?" She looked concerned, but not crushed. She obviously wasn't going to give up hope easily.

"Sure. I need to check on the Littledale bridge, too, which you'd have to cross on the route out." He grimaced. "It goes down at least once every winter. Not exactly an engineering marvel."

She smiled. "Can you call now?"

"Soon." He stood up. "Before that, though, I'd like you to see this. You came up here to negotiate this deal, and we'd better get that out of the way first, don't you think?"

Crossing to the sofa, he handed her the legal pad, on which he had outlined the terms he was willing to offer Robert Hamilton. She took it with a quizzical expression, which turned to astonishment as she read the items scrawled there.

Daniel propped himself on the edge of the desk, waiting for the significance of the information to sink in. That expression told him that she had no trouble deciphering his handwriting. And why should she? He remembered that her manager had described her as an excellent stenographer.

"But this—" She dropped the pad onto her lap. "This says you will buy the company."

He nodded. "There are some clarifications, of course, a couple of adjustments in the terms—"

"But they're *nothing*!" She picked up the pad again, as if to confirm what seemed impossible. "I mean, they're such small things. You know Robert will gladly agree to them." She stared at him, her eyes confused and somehow skeptical. "Essentially, what this boils down to is that you'll buy the company."

He nodded again.

"But why?" She put her hand in her hair, which was loose this morning, and massaged her head, apparently trying to force her thoughts into some coherent order. She swung her legs down, her bare feet pale against the multicolored carpet, and sat up, as if better posture would make for better cognition.

He suddenly noticed that she was wearing one of Doreen's outfits—a pair of jeans cinched with Lindsay's own belt to compensate for her slightly narrower waist, and the least outlandish of the Cheyenne Queen's beaded T-shirts. Funny how different the same clothes could look on two women, he thought. The turquoise and silver suited Lindsay's dark hair and blue eyes remarkably well.

"Don't ask why, Lindsay. Haven't you ever been taught the cardinal rule of salesmanship? Once you get your 'yes,' stop talking."

"Two days ago you said there was only a one in a million chance."

"Maybe you're just a terrific salesman."

She flushed. "Don't patronize me, Mr. McKinley."

So they were back to "Mr. McKinley," were they? He wondered whether it was the business nature of the conversation or Robert's jealous protestations that had put an end to their artificial intimacy. Or maybe it was just the weather—and the prospect of escape. Her eagerness to leave this mountain was decidedly unflattering.

"All right, I won't," he said, dropping the smile. He reached out and flicked the stereo off. The Christmas bells vanished, as if a huge hand had smothered them.

"I have very sound financial reasons for buying Hamilton Homes," he said. "Half a dozen analysts and lawyers back in Phoenix have been crunching numbers for me over the past two weeks, and the bottom line is I think I can turn this development around."

She narrowed her eyes, clearly unconvinced and still suspicious. Daniel could see her mind whirring behind the tight, thoughtful expression, but she knew he wasn't fool enough to say more. If he was the only one who had nosed that corporate relocation rumor out, well, that was simply his good fortune. He'd found out legally— he never stooped to hiring spies or paying bribes—and he, by God, wasn't morally required to pass the information to Hamilton by way of his Madonna-faced girlfriend.

So, frustrated, she just sat there, her blue eyes dark, her finger squeezing the notepad. He suspected she would have preferred to have her pretty hands around his neck instead. Good thing she would be leaving soon. If she got any more stressed, he might have to sleep with his back to the wall. He smiled at the mental image of Lindsay creeping into his bedroom, dressed in Doreen's beads and feathers, tomahawk in hand.

She must have misinterpreted his smile, because her darkened eyes flashed like lightning out of a stormy sky. "Look, Mr. McKinley—" she began heatedly.

Luckily, Roc chose that moment to come stomping down from the second floor, his arms full of cardboard boxes.

"Coming through!" He lurched toward the sofa, barely able to see around the boxes. "Stand aside!"

"What now?" Taking advantage of the distraction, Daniel eased the legal pad from Lindsay's tense fingers. Walking back to the desk, he tore off the top page and began feeding the sheet into the fax machine. He wanted to buy Hamilton Homes. He didn't intend to let Lindsay's personal dislike for him foul up the negotiations. She didn't want that, either, and she wouldn't be risking it if she weren't so frustrated by this whole blizzard disaster. She had come here to help Robert Hamilton, and she would leave here with a contract in hand.

"Roc," he said dryly as he programmed the fax to make the call. "Please tell me that those aren't more Pocahontas costumes."

Boxes tumbled to the empty side of the sofa as Roc finally let go of his burden. "You mean, Doreen's stuff? Nah, she must have taken all her feathered headdresses with her."

He peeled open one of the flaps and, after rustling through tissue paper for several seconds, held up a glittering red ball like a trophy. "Better than that, boss. See? I've found the Christmas decorations. Miss Lindsay here was noticing that we didn't have any, so I went up to the attic to look. See, she just may be leaving this afternoon, if the wind dies down, but she promised to help me put them up before she goes."

Roc reached out to switch the stereo back on. As the bells again began to peal, he batted his white lashes in a ridiculous parody of innocent candor. "Didn't you promise to help us, Miss Lindsay?"

"Of course I will." But Lindsay's answering smile was strained, as if she now regretted having promised anything that would keep her in this lodge another minute.

Daniel slowly punched in the last of his secretary's fax numbers. The machine obediently began its weird electronic babbling, but it was drowned out by the extravagant sound of Christmas bells and the insistent whine of the wind.

"So we'll be able to spruce this dump up for Christmas after all. Great news, huh, boss?"

Daniel counted to ten before he said anything. When he did speak, he kept his voice low.

"Amazing news." He stared straight into Roc's brown eyes. He'd never heard such humbug. Roc knew damn well that Daniel never decorated for Christmas anymore. To Daniel, Christmas meant nothing but loss. No Santa could ever bring back what Christmas had taken away from him three years ago. "I thought you had thrown those things away." He tightened his voice. "As I told you to do."

"Why, yes, I thought so, too!" Roc raised his brows so high in feigned astonishment that they all but disappeared into his wild mane. "It's just amazing, boss. I don't know *what* happened. I must have mistaken them for more of the Indian Princess's things, I guess. I know these decorations are old, but we just let the time get away from us and forgot to buy new ones, didn't we? And now, just when we need some, here they are! Can you believe it?"

"No." Daniel almost had to admire the old man's nerve. Did he really think that, just because Lindsay was here as a witness, Daniel wouldn't wring his neck for this? "I don't think I can."

Roc's eyes glazed over as he fondled the ornament reverently.

"It may be a miracle, boss," he said in hushed, pious tones. "A hot-damn, card-carrying Christmas miracle."

* * *

An hour later Lindsay was standing at the top of the staircase, helping Roc measure the banister for a pine branch garland, wishing she had never mentioned Christmas decorations at all. At the time, she had been feeling charitable toward Daniel McKinley—intoxicated, no doubt, by the sight of the clear, snowless sky—and it had seemed terribly sad to her that he had let his tragedy rob the holiday of its special spirit of hope.

It had been three years, after all. Wasn't it time to stop dwelling on the heartbreak and let some of the good memories back in? He had been married for eight years, and his little girl had been at least six—there must have been many Christmases that were warm with love and laughter. What about the puppies with blue bows around their necks, the bicycles that wouldn't go together right, the absurd, hideous ties from a crazy old uncle? What about the kisses beneath the mistletoe?

Three years ago. Lindsay's own Christmas that year had been particularly painful, too. Her father had died only two months before. She and Christy, who was only nine at the time, were struggling with the agonizing loneliness of being orphans. Her grandparents were threatening to take Christy away from her. And, to top it all, she had just been fired, two days before Christmas.

She could have retreated into a bitter resentment against the holiday that seemed such a mockery of her own grim reality. But instead she had decided she owed it to Christy to carry on with as much courage as she could find.

Daniel's loss had been much greater, of course, but didn't he, too, owe it to the memory of his wife and child to focus on the good times? Should one tragic day permanently erase all the joy they had known together?

At least that was what she had thought this morning. Now she didn't really care *what* Daniel McKinley did about Christmas, she thought as she anchored the measuring tape against the top newel, waiting while Roc walked it down along the curved wooden banister. Every day of Daniel's life could be Halloween for all she cared.

"Oh, drat and damnation!" Roc had reached the bottom of the stairs and clearly didn't like the number he saw on the tape measure. "I *knew* I should have saved those artificial garlands. Jocelyn had reams of 'em, all Victorian foofy stuff loaded down with lace and pearls and trash like that. I hated the things, but I miss 'em now. I'm going to be cutting branches until Valentine's Day to cover this whole blasted staircase."

Lindsay could see the problem. "Do you have any popcorn?" she asked, musing. She had seen a huge bucket of pinecones in one corner of the great room, and it had given her an idea. "And any old red cloth you don't need?"

Roc screwed up his eyebrows, obviously thinking hard. "I always keep a ton of popcorn around during the blizzard season," he said wryly, "but red cloth..." His eyes widened, and he held up his index finger jubilantly. "Eureka," he exclaimed. "I have an old red tablecloth I had planned to cut up for rags. Why do you ask? Do you have a plan that doesn't involve me standing for hours rump-deep in the snow? If you do, I'll love you forever." He grinned. "You'll be my Christmas angel."

Lindsay shook the measuring tape impatiently. The metallic wave rippled down to Roc's hand, a slow, slithering reprimand. His nonsensical flirtation had grown even more outrageous over the past hour, ever since Daniel had left the two of them alone to handle the decorating.

"Hush now," she said. "I really do have an idea. One year the PTA at Christy's school decorated the stairwells for Christmas. PTAs never have much money, you know, so we had to improvise. We used little clusters of pine-cones and popcorn that dangled from big red bows every couple of feet or so."

She smiled, remembering how she had enjoyed the meetings, at which mothers and fathers—and, of course, one big sister—had sat together, discussing the curriculum and child-rearing, while they strung popcorn and tied bows. Though it had been hard to find the time, Lindsay had always been active in the PTA. She learned so much from those other men and women, who had welcomed her warmly and helped her through so many little crises.

"I love it," Roc said, immediately supportive. "But it sounds like a lot of work, and I'm not going to be much use tying bows one-handed. God knows old Scrooge McKinley won't be pitching in. Do you think you'll have time to do it?"

Daniel's door opened at that moment, and for a second he just stood in the doorway watching them, a powerful black shadow against the bright light from his window. He had been making calls, checking on the chances for an escape this afternoon. Lindsay held her breath at the sight of him, waiting for his verdict.

"I'm afraid she has all the time she could possibly need," he said, sending her hopes tumbling in a breath-taking descent into disappointment. Only now, when she knew she couldn't leave, did she understand how much she had wanted to go home.

"The news is as bad as it could be," Daniel continued. "The bridge is down. The roads are buried. A few emergency vehicles are getting through, but they say they have too many real emergencies to bother with us as long as we have heat and food and water."

He turned to Lindsay, who could hardly breathe. "I'm sorry," he said. "Getting you home for Christmas just isn't very high on their list."

Lindsay leaned back in her chair and stretched her aching back. It had been a long, lonely afternoon. Roc and Daniel were up on the roof, clearing away heavy loads of snow from the few areas that weren't pitched properly and tended to let the icy weight pile up dangerously. She had been inside all day, listening halfheartedly to Christmas carols, popping corn by the bushel and tying these red bows, which somehow didn't have the same merry cheer as the ones she'd made with the PTA.

Now the wicker basket on the floor beside her was half full with huge red bows, and her fingers were stiff from twisting the strips around themselves. She sat in the kitchen, which was still the brightest room in the house, even though it was very late, nearly time to fix dinner. The white tiles around her were stained strawberry by the setting sun.

She wished she could shake this mournful feeling that had settled over her spirits. It wasn't like her—she rarely gave in to depression, no matter what happened. She had long ago decided that she'd use the good advise her mother had given her—that way, she could make her life a sort of personal memorial to her mother, who had been a remarkable woman. "Don't fight life, Linney," her mother had said, using that sweet firm voice Lindsay had loved so much. "If you've got to do a thing, do it with a smile."

But today she couldn't find a smile anywhere. She was unshakably sad. And, though she was ashamed of the feeling, she was also inexplicably, unfairly *angry*. She knew Daniel McKinley hadn't ordered the bad weather just to hurt her, but somehow he was the target for her resentment anyway.

Not that he cared. After giving her the bad news, he had turned away from her disappointment casually, simply shrugging his broad shoulders into his down-filled jacket and calling to Roc to come help him with the roof. Self-centered, shallow...

But the worst thing was that, in spite of her resentment—or perhaps as a perverse outgrowth of it— she found him disturbingly attractive. Physically, only, of course. Other than those gorgeous eyes, sexy body and curious animal magnetism, he had nothing she wanted. No heart, and no soul.

Why, then, did her breathing tighten slightly whenever he walked into the room? Why did she think back on that night so often, the night when she had found him alone in the dark, turning the chess piece over and over in his hands? Why did she feel a little funny whenever she thought of those hands at all?

It must be the peculiar, artificial domesticity creating an illusion in her befuddled brain. She had read stories of kidnapped women falling in love with their captors, or POWs becoming best friends with their guards. Yes, that must be it. Daniel McKinley was hardly her type in *real* life. If only she could get back to real life before she forgot what it was like—and who she was when she was living it!

Lindsay looked down at the bow she was tying. It looked more like a dead red snake. Picking apart the knot, she cursed under her breath. If she were stuck in this house until Christmas, she was going to cover every square inch with these blasted red bows. Let him try to pretend it wasn't Christmas then!

She had just begun to retie the hapless shank of satin when she heard a muffled voice call her name.

"Lindsay!" It was a man's voice, though the moaning wind made it impossible to be sure whether it was Daniel or Roc. The voice sounded hoarse, as if it might have been calling for a long time. "Lindsay..." The sound grew fainter, until she wasn't sure whether she heard a man or just the wind.

"Come," she thought it said. "Help."

CHAPTER FIVE

A MAN'S jacket hung on a peg by the kitchen door, and Lindsay grabbed it, only half conscious of doing so, as she darted out. She rushed through the utility room, then into the woodshed, and from there out into the side yard, her feet sinking deep into the soft, new-fallen snow.

"Daniel!" The syllables seemed to be torn out of her mouth by the wind and hurled away before her own ears could hear them. She called again, praying that the men could hear what she could not. "Roc! Daniel!"

She was completely unprepared for the wild force of the wind, which yanked her hair and sent it flying in all directions. The bitterly cold gusts swept through Doreen's nonsensical T-shirt as if it had been made of tissue paper. Startled, Lindsay yanked the jacket shut, fumbling at the zipper with stiff fingers that already felt half frozen. She dug into the pockets and found a pair of men's gloves, which she put on gratefully.

"Over here!"

Lindsay looked up, toward the roof over the kitchen, from where the words had seemed to be coming. But the wind must have been playing tricks with sound. That bit of roof wore a layer of snow as smooth and unmarred as a fresh coat of white paint. Roc and Daniel clearly had not been up there at all today.

She hesitated, cupping her hand around her ear, trying to block the roar of the wind long enough to hear the voice again. But standing still was not a good idea. She could feel herself sinking slowly as the fresh snow packed down under her weight. With light, careful steps, she circled toward the back of the house, never taking her eyes from the roof.

"Daniel?" She felt suddenly disoriented. Everything out here was so strangely blank, all white, disfiguring drifts that camouflaged everything that ought to be familiar. The strawberry sunset was dying, the light growing gray. Was this the office side of the house? Or was she near the kitchen again? How many corners had she turned?

"Lindsay!" The voice was strained, but it was clearly Daniel's. "Up here!"

When her searching, frantic gaze finally found them, she put her hands to her mouth to hold back a cry of dismay. Roc lay sprawled beside the chimney, facedown, as if he were sleeping. But, horribly, his body was nearly upside down, his arms dangling over the edge of the gableboard. For a confused, terrified moment Lindsay couldn't understand why he hadn't fallen.

Then she saw Daniel, who was squatting against the back of the chimney, holding on to Rock's legs with both hands. Roc's weight was clearly pulling him down—even as she watched the body slid another two inches, and snow rained down from the roof below him.

"Oh, my God," she whispered into her frozen fingers. "Roc."

"Lindsay!" Daniel turned his face, so that his profile was just barely visible around the chimney. "Do you see the ladder?"

She tore her terrified gaze from the long black form on the roof and scanned the eaves.

"Yes," she called, her voice strange and hoarse. Her throat felt frozen, too. "Yes, I see it!" A very long extension ladder, opened up all the way, was several feet to her left, leaning against the roofline like a silver staircase.

"Can you bring it closer?"

"Yes." She tried not to shiver, but it was brutally cold out here. She wondered how long Daniel and Roc had been up there, calling for her.

Though the metal was so icy it almost burned through the gloves, she managed to move the ladder until it was just inches from where Roc's hand dangled. She rested it gingerly against the edge of the roof, afraid to jar the precarious balance that Daniel had so desperately achieved.

"I got it," she called up, hoping she had done the right thing. Daniel's urgent instructions were so terse.

"Good. I'm going to need your help, Lindsay, if I'm going to get him down. Now can you climb up far enough to reach his shoulders?"

"I think so." She looked up, swallowing hard. Several feet over her head, Roc's limp hand swayed in the clutch of the cruel wind. It was oddly blue, like a dead hand, and the sight made her feel slightly sick. Of course Roc was not dead, she told herself. She had seen death come before, but only for people whose bodies were worn out with sickness, like her mother, or with misery, like her father. She couldn't even imagine death claiming someone as vital as Roc.

She put her foot on the bottom rung and gasped as the ladder shifted under her weight. "Daniel," she cried. "The ladder is sinking."

"It's all right," he called down, his voice strangely bracing. "It's only going to sink about a foot. Then you'll hit older snow. It's harder, like ice. Go ahead, Lindsay. You can do it."

She tried to take a deep breath, but coughed as the frigid air seared her lungs. Her eyes watered, and she wiped the moisture away with the back of her hand.

Blinking, she focused herself, staring at the ladder as if she could will it to help her.

Shutting her eyes, she put all her weight on the rung and waited until she could feel the legs settle on firm footing. And then she opened her eyes and began to climb. One, two, three, four...she counted the steps, never taking her gaze from Roc's helpless hand.

Finally she was at roof level, and her own fears were forgotten as she saw the horrible red stain in the snow around Roc's head. Roc... She bent over him, touching his face, which felt frighteningly cold and stiff. She looked up, her heart pounding. "Daniel?"

"He'll be all right." Daniel's voice was harsh, as if he were defying anyone to disagree. "He slipped, and he hit his head on the chimney. Thank God, I was close enough to catch his legs before he fell."

"Yes," she said. "Yes."

"I can get him down, but I need you to hold his shoulders so that he doesn't slip until I can get back with another ladder." He twisted as far as he could, and his eyes bored into hers. "Can you do that?"

"Yes." She didn't know if she could or not, but that was the only answer possible. "I can do that."

"Good." He shifted, as if his position were uncomfortable. Lindsay wondered if his legs had grown numb, squatting that way for so long. Guilt assaulted her like a new blast of wind. How long had he been there before she heard him? Would his stiff legs be able to move nimbly, safely, when they had to?

"Now press your whole body against the line of the roof." Her fear must have been in her eyes, because he nodded firmly. "Yes. Do it. The ladder won't slip, and it will give you balance."

She leaned into the fascia board. Her breasts just cleared the roof and pressed into the snow, which fell all around the ladder, reminding her of how far away the ground was. But Daniel was right. She did feel more secure.

"Now lean over him, all the way, that's right...and shove the heels of your hands against his shoulders. Push hard, Lindsay. Harder. The snow has melted around him, and it's made a depression that's helping to hold him. I don't think he's going to fall any farther right now, but I don't want to take any chances."

She shivered. She hoped Daniel was right. The thought of Roc's massive body tumbling forward, like a terrible black avalanche slamming into her, knocking her off the ladder, was enough to make her stomach begin to swim. She shut her eyes, bowed her head, and pushed with all her might.

"Excellent," Daniel said. "Now just hold on. I'm going to go down across the kitchen roof. It's lower." He paused. "I'll be back as quickly as I can."

"I know you will." She didn't open her eyes. "Be careful."

He seemed to be gone an eternity. It was like being stranded on an empty, frozen planet. It would be full night soon. There was no motion but the churning of the trees. No sound but the whine of the wind, which would occasionally send a flurry of snow drifting over them, as if it wanted to obliterate them as it had obliterated everything else. Soon Roc's black jacket was almost white, her gloved hands were buried to the wrist, and still Daniel had not returned.

She wouldn't let herself be afraid. She talked to Roc softly the whole time, telling him what had happened, reassuring him that Daniel would soon be back, that everything would be fine. She had no idea whether Roc heard her or not, but it made her feel a little less alone.

And then Daniel was there. She felt rather than heard the scrape of another ladder being propped on the roof right next to hers. She expected to see Daniel climbing up beside her, but to her shock she felt a trembling in her own ladder, and suddenly he was right behind her.

His body was pressed so tightly against hers that he blocked the wind and she felt a sudden surge of blessed warmth. He must have been on the step just below her. When he spoke his voice was so close to her ear that she could feel the misting of his breath against her cheek.

"I'm here, Lindsay," he said softly. "It's going to be all right."

A shameful weakening spread through her limbs, and she had the sudden urge to cry. It was just the relief, she knew, the sweet relief of not being alone anymore, but she hated the way her body sagged against his. He put his arms around her, and pressed himself even closer.

"It's all right," he said again. "You did it." He held her a moment, and then he slid his arm under hers and put his gloved hand over hers on Roc's shoulders. "All right, now, this is a little tricky, but you can do it. I want you to put your left foot on the new ladder. I'll hold it steady. I'll take over holding Roc, and you can shift your other foot to the new ladder, too. Then I want you to climb down. Carefully."

When she didn't speak, he nudged her with his shoulder. "Do you understand, Lindsay? Can you do it?"

"Yes," she said, because again that was the only answer. Some cowardly, irrational part of her didn't want to leave the protection of his warm body and his strong arms. But she couldn't give in to that. Roc needed help. He needed to be brought down from this snowy roof and stretched out by the fire. Then maybe, just maybe, the blue would leave his lips and he would open his eyes

again. Yes, she could do it, would do it, because she
had to.

And she did. Foot over foot, with Daniel tossing gentle
encouragement every step of the way. "Good girl," he
said softly as she finally reached the safety of the ground.
"Good job."

Paradoxically, now that they were on firm ground,
her legs began to shake, and she leaned against the rough
bark of a ponderosa pine to support herself. She was so
glad, so very glad, to be off that ladder.

Her relief was short-lived. Looking up, she realized
the most dangerous part of the rescue was still to come.
Her blood running slow and glacial in her veins, she
watched as Daniel dragged Roc's body toward him. He
was miraculously managing to keep his balance even as
the bigger man's weight fell forward onto his shoulder.
Snow tumbled around him in chunks, and the imprint
of Roc's body was left behind where the snow had melted
beneath him.

Oh, God, it seemed impossible. She held her breath
and laced her gloved fingers into tight braids of fear.
Daniel backed slowly down the ladder, taking more and
more of Roc's limp body as he went. He would fall,
surely he would fall, and they both would die.

But he didn't fall. Finally, with Roc draped across his
shoulders in a position she'd only seen during a televised
fire rescue, Daniel was taking the last three steps, holding
on to the ladder with one hand.

Tears froze on her face as his feet finally found the
ground. She ran to him, clutching his sleeve with her
gloved hand. She tried to speak, but there were no words,
only the tears that froze as quickly as they fell. One small
sob of relief escaped her trembling lips.

"Hush, Lindsay," he said quietly, speaking with the same comforting tenderness he might have shown to a fearful child. "It's all over now."

Half an hour later, she was kneeling by the sofa, where Daniel had deposited Roc carefully, stretching Roc's long frame into a position so natural that, if she hadn't known better, she might have thought he'd settled himself for a nap in front of the fire.

Together they had placed an emergency call to 9-1-1, alerting the rescue people to Roc's condition, and they had bandaged the cut on his head.

After that Daniel had immediately sent her upstairs to change her clothes. While she was gone he had, she saw, removed Roc's wet things and redressed him in a dry set of clothes. Watching the firelight play over Roc's massive body, Lindsay couldn't help wondering at the strength that allowed Daniel to maneuver him with such apparent ease.

Daniel was upstairs changing, now, too. Trying not to think about that, Lindsay toweled Roc's long white hair, smoothing it back from his face as gently as she could so that she didn't press against the cut, which was surrounded by a bruise that seemed to grow more deep and purple with every passing second.

He hadn't awakened, though the warmth of the fire had brought a more normal color to his skin, and his pulse, thank God, was strong. She pressed her forefingers to his wrist and checked again, though she had done so four times already in the past half hour.

Asleep like this and helpless, Roc looked much older. The contrast was painful. What a force his personality carried! Awake, he was timeless. Unconscious, he was an old man.

Just then, she heard Daniel come down the stairs, but she didn't look up, unwilling to let him glimpse the tears that shimmered in front of her eyes. She knew he wasn't a man who would tolerate much weakness, and she'd already exhibited enough out there on the ladder.

"Any change?" He sat on the edge of the sofa, close enough for his knee to graze her elbow, and touched Roc's cheek with the back of his hand. "He's warming up. That's good."

"He hasn't stirred at all," she said, tilting on her heels. The movement put a few more inches between them, though it brought her uncomfortably close to the fire.

She suddenly felt much too warm in Doreen's soft gray suede dress. It was an awful dress, each long sleeve studded with jade and silver medallions the size of quarters. Even worse, it fit her poorly, especially in the bust. Doreen must have been extremely... Lindsay picked at the loose material self-consciously, trying to picture her. Extremely buxom.

Daniel, of course, looked as elegant as ever, though he didn't appear to have gone to any great pains to accomplish the effect. He had changed into a teal flannel shirt and black corduroy trousers that were clearly well-worn, and he hadn't even taken the time to dry his hair, which licked wetly at the curve of his ear.

She averted her gaze from the sight, only to find herself looking down at the way the rows of corduroy followed the muscles in his leg. She stood up abruptly. Didn't the man own a single thing that wasn't fatally flattering? *Oh, Roc*, she thought, *if only you knew how much I need you!* She had already grown so fond of his barbaric humor and paradoxically sweet smile, and so dependent on his help in dealing with Daniel.

But Roc didn't know—and perhaps he never would. He was still heartbreakingly pale, and his breathing was loud and labored. Barely able to stand the fears that tortured her, Lindsay began to pace helplessly. The rescue people had said that, because the blizzard had so over-burdened their resources, they couldn't possibly send anyone out to pick up Roc until tomorrow. Twelve whole hours to wait, then, at the very least. She had to get hold of herself. She couldn't let her anxiety swallow her whole.

Daniel looked over at her, watching her pace for a moment, and then he put his hand on Roc's shoulder.

"Come on, Roc, old man," he said. "Time to wake up."

Lindsay stopped and stared at him, amazed. His tone was perfectly normal, full of the same teasing irreverence he always showed toward Roc. He didn't sound worried at all.

"Come on, buddy," he said. "You can hear me. You're not going to turn into a wimp-guts on me now, are you?"

"Wimp-guts?" Lindsay broke in, unable to bear Roc's answering silence any longer. Her voice was as taut as a bowstring, and, though she hadn't intended for them to, the words shot out like arrows. "That's a little much, isn't it? I hardly think he can be accused of cowardice."

She flushed, suddenly aware of how contentious she sounded. And it obviously wasn't just her imagination. Daniel's brows went up, and his hand froze on Roc's shoulder.

"Oh?" he said with a deadly calm. "Really?"

"Yes, really." Though she tried to loosen the pinched tone, she wasn't very successful. Her throat felt too tight, as if someone were squeezing her vocal cords. "Look at him! He's—didn't you say he was seventy-four years old?"

Daniel nodded, a slow motion that sent fire glow sliding across his damp hair.

"Seventy-four! And yet he was up on that roof, wasn't he?" Lindsay gestured toward the high-beamed ceiling. "Risking his life to help you shovel snow. Couldn't you have stopped him? You must have known that he—"

She pressed her hand over her eyes, trying to blot out the memory of the sprawled black form, the ominous red stain in the perfect white blanket of snow. She had been so frightened by the sight. She was even more frightened now.

Suddenly claustrophobic from the sultry heat of the fireplace, she shoved her sleeves up to her elbows and prowled restlessly toward the picture window. She stared out at the floodlit white world, biting her lower lip, trying to keep from venting her nerves in more belligerent words.

"Roc wanted to do it, Lindsay." Daniel's voice was so low, so calm, that her own seemed to echo shrilly by comparison. "Surely you've noticed how proud he is. He can't bear feeling helpless."

It was true, at least partly. She knew it was.

"But you could have stopped him," she argued, driven in spite of herself to press the point. "You're the one who's responsible. You're the boss."

He didn't answer at first, his hand still on Roc's shoulder. She knew by his studied calm that he was angry. It frightened her, but, perversely, she was in the mood for a fight, ready after these three long years to speak some of the bitter things that she'd so far only said to herself.

Even more importantly, an open clash would put her firmly back in an adversarial relationship with him. She was comfortable with pure antagonism, but these other, newer feelings were much more ambivalent. And just plain unnerving.

Some softening of her attitude had been inevitable, she supposed, living this way with him—sleeping under the same roof, eating at the same table, warming themselves at the same fire. And then, tonight, the intimate physical cooperation that had been required to rescue Roc.

In all those things lurked a subtle sexual component, and it had led to this miserable hyper-awareness of Daniel as a man. It had reduced her to this unhealthy obsession with the colors, textures and fit of his clothing, the warmth and scent of his gloves, the curling blue-black highlights of his hair.

She shivered, though she stood only two feet from the blazing fire. No, she'd much rather fight.

"Are you sure it's pride? Maybe it's fear," she went on boldly. "Maybe Roc just is afraid to let you see that he can't do it all anymore. Maybe if you were a little more sensitive to what *his* needs are, if you understood him, accepted his fear—"

"Understood him?" Daniel's eyes flashed a blue as icy as moonlight on the snow. "Let me get this straight. Are you implying that I need *you* to help me understand a man I've known for thirty years?"

"No." She straightened her back, steeling herself against the biting sarcasm in his question. It did, indeed, seem preposterous to presume that, on two days' acquaintance, she could know Roc better than he did. But the autocratic self-absorption that she had seen in Daniel three years ago was the same insensitivity that made him blind to Roc's weakness now.

The memory had been well-timed to reinforce her courage. She set her jaw. "I'm not *implying* anything, actually. I'm saying this straight out. You need help understanding not just Roc, but all human frailty. I've worked for you before, remember? I know that you have unreasonably high expectations of the people you employ. Sometimes those people just can't meet those expectations, though since most of them are completely dependent on your paycheck, they will try to. And try, and try, and try, until—''

She heard her voice climbing as her emotions began to outstrip her common sense. She stopped, took a deep breath, and waved her hand toward Roc's helpless body. "And that can lead to tragedy."

To her surprise, Daniel didn't respond with the immediate backlash she had feared. Instead he stood up, walked to the bar on the other side of the hearth, and poured out a snifter of something amber that sparkled in the firelight. He came back and, without a smile, handed it to her. She took it, equally unsmiling.

He gave her hand a small nudge. "Drink it. It might make you feel better."

"It won't," she said stiffly, feeling somehow patronized. Was he writing her off as hysterical, emotionally unhinged by the traumatic day? How convenient for him! If she was just an overwrought female, he could still refuse to face the truth about himself.

"The only thing that will make me feel better," she insisted, "is if Roc regains consciousness."

He sighed. "We both want that, Lindsay." Wearily, he sat on one of the armchairs, settling comfortably in its depths. Lifting one elbow, he propped his head against his knuckles and looked up at her, his eyes glittering in the firelight. "But the truth is that we're not really talking about Roc here anymore, are we?"

"Of course we are." She swallowed a mouthful of the drink, forgetting that she had decided she wouldn't. She needed it. She was feeling a little shaky suddenly, as her emotion that had fueled her a moment ago drained away. She shouldn't have picked this fight if she didn't have the stamina to finish it. "And we're talking about you, too. The way you drive your employees."

"Right. Well, let's do it, then. Sit down." He pointed to the other armchair, which was angled toward his, with only a small honeywood table and the ivory chess set between them. He looked surprised when she didn't obey. "Please," he added perfunctorily.

She took another swig of the liquid, which tasted like honey that had been set on fire. She eased herself onto the edge of the armchair. "All right," she said, folding her hands in her lap, the brandy snifter nestled between her laced thumbs.

"You've always disliked me, haven't you?" He made the blunt statement impassively, as if the idea didn't bother him much. He sounded merely curious, as if such a thing didn't happen very often. "Right from the start."

"No," she said slowly. "Not always. When I first went to work for you, I thought you were..." She stalled, sipping the brandy, wondering how much she should say. This whole conversation didn't seem quite real, and it was hard to tell where the boundaries ought to be. "I admired you very much. Everyone said you were the best."

She relaxed into her chair a little, warmed by the brandy and the crackling fire. She felt good about that answer. It was the truth, if not the whole truth. He didn't need to hear how everyone in the steno pool had drooled over the good-looking young tycoon who ruled from the regal splendor of the tenth floor. He wasn't a warm and fuzzy boss, the kind who dropped by merely to raise morale or to distribute the Christmas bonuses, but his inaccessibility had only contributed to the mystique. He seemed glamorous, as rare and exciting as a comet.

Some of the most smitten secretaries had arrived early and stayed late, cherishing the remote dream of riding

the same elevator as Daniel McKinley, who was famous
for keeping gruelling hours. They grilled the middle
managers, who had more generous access to the boss,
for details.

The day Daniel brought his daughter to a board
meeting, for instance, had been the stuff of legend.
Lindsay had heard how the adorable Alice had sat to
her father's right, and she had been given a legal pad to
draw on while the board members took their notes. She
had even heard about the yellow crinoline under the little
girl's blue dotted swiss dress.

Remembering the buzz of gossip that day, Lindsay
suddenly realized that the other secretaries would
probably kill to change places with her now. She didn't
know why that hadn't occurred to her sooner. Daniel
didn't even seem like that same remote, mysterious
symbol of oppression anymore. He had become disturbingly real.

Still, Felicia and Janine in particular would think she
was crazy to be so eager to leave. She tilted the snifter
to her lips and drained another quarter of an inch. Ironic,
wasn't it? And tough luck for Daniel. The one woman
who wouldn't puddle at his feet was the one he got
stranded with.

"So when did all that change?" Daniel's gaze had
never faltered from her face, though she realized there
must have been a long silence. "I like to think I'm as
good a businessman as I ever was, and yet obviously you
quit admiring me quite some time ago."

She raised her glass in a mocking salute. "Well, you
did fire me, remember?"

"I also remember why." He smiled evenly. "So it
seems to me that your opinion must have changed
somewhat prior to that."

"It happened gradually, I think," she said, trying for a calm candor. It would be less easy for him to dismiss her if she didn't rant. "You paid well, but you were terribly inflexible. We were all scared to death of you, did you know that? We used to lie for one another, covering for a secretary whose kid was sick, or a clerk who was late because her car broke down. We all knew that you didn't give anyone much leeway."

"Most big companies are strict about things like that, Lindsay." He still didn't seem to care, really, what she thought. He seemed to offer the statement simply as an interesting fact. "They have to be to stay solvent."

"Robert's not at all strict," she said without thinking. "He's always been completely understanding when anyone has a problem. You always know he'll let you have whatever time you need."

She knew even before she heard him laugh that she had stupidly walked right into the trap.

"And Hamilton Homes is a financial nightmare," he said wryly. "I rest my case."

"Well, perhaps he is too lenient. I've admitted that before." She twisted her brandy glass, watching the liquid splash, a small storm in the large, rounded bowl. Catching the hot glow of the fire, it was a lot like the churning resentment trapped in her breast, she thought. She drank some more, enjoying the image.

"But even if Robert's way is folly, shouldn't there be some happy medium?" She looked over at him, feeling much braver now. "Isn't there a management style somewhere between the pushover who lets his business go under and the slave driver who would break up a family rather than let one of his secretaries work a few hours each day from home?"

"Work from home?" Daniel lowered his arm slowly, straightening his head so that he could watch her carefully. "I don't know what you're talking about," he said in a low, controlled voice. "Break up whose family?"

Now it was her turn to laugh. "What do you mean, you don't know? Mine, of course. You're the one who told me I couldn't work at home, even for two hours a day. I had worked for the McKinley Corporation for two full years without missing a single day, without ever asking for any special considerations of any kind."

She narrowed her eyes. "But that didn't carry any weight with you, did it? You didn't give a damn that my parents had both died that year. You didn't give a damn that my grandparents were suing for custody of my sister—"

Her voice broke slightly, but she toughened it immediately and went on. "And they would have gotten her, too, if I hadn't been able to prove that I could earn a living and still be at home when she got out of school each day. Robert did that for me, Daniel." Her eyes stung and watered, remembering. "*Robert*. Not you."

Daniel leaned forward and took the brandy from her trembling fingers. "Lindsay, you're not making sense. I didn't even know your name until the day I—until the day you left my company. I had never set eyes on you before."

She crossed her arms over her chest. "Well, your Mr. Browder certainly knew me. Remember him? He was the coldhearted reptile who ran your steno pool." She raised one corner of her mouth in what she hoped was a sneer, but her lips felt queerly numb. "I'm sure he's still there. You'd never fire someone whose managerial style is so close to your own, would you? In fact, I'd bet you've promoted him."

She was thrilled to see an uneasy look cross Daniel's face. She had hit the target with that one, hadn't she? If it was actually possible that he had not monitored

Browder's activities, that he had given that horrible man carte blanche with the lives of all those hapless secretaries...well, it was high time he realized what Browder was doing with all his unchecked authority.

"Browder did come to me several times," Daniel said slowly, as if he were thinking about something long ago and far away, something that was shrouded in a haze of incomplete memories. "I remember him saying that he was having trouble with some of the secretaries. They were abusing the leave guidelines, or..." He shook his head. "Or something like that. I really can't remember the details."

"And what did you say?"

Daniel shrugged. "I'm sure I told him to handle it however he saw fit. It was his department. I don't micromanage my executives. It's bad business."

"Much better to be oblivious, of course." Her voice was laced with scorn. "Better to hire someone to keep the peons in line, keep the slaves working, turning the wheel that makes more money for you. That way you don't ever have to think that those little pawns in your corporate game are real people, with real problems."

She leaned her head back, suddenly tired from the expenditure of angry energy. "Well, no wonder Browder was so heartless. The attitudes of any company filter down from the top, don't they?"

He didn't answer. But she could imagine what he was thinking. Oh, well...at least it was all out in the open now. But she was surprised that the return to enemy status didn't give her any more satisfaction. She felt tired, and queerly empty, as if venting the resentment she'd nursed all these years had drained her of all emotion.

With a long sigh, she stood up, amazed that her legs were as steady as they were. "Which brings us back where we started, I think. To Roc. He's a wonderful man who's grappling with his age and his infirmities, and probably is afraid to tell you about them. But he shouldn't *have* to tell you. You should be able to sense them on your own. That's all I wanted to say."

Ignoring the way Daniel watched her silently from his icy silver-blue eyes, she opened the Indian blanket that had been folded over the back of the sofa. Carefully she spread its bright colors over Roc's sleeping body.

"One of us should watch him all night," she said as crisply as her numb lips would allow. "Do you want to take the first shift or the second?"

"Neither." The word was firm. "You need to sleep."

"I can't," she said, touching Roc's cheek in a lingering good-night. She turned and walked toward the staircase. "I'll take the second shift, then, if you don't mind," she said over her shoulder. "I'll set the alarm for three."

"I appreciate the offer, Lindsay." His voice was formal, reflecting the immense gulf that lay once again between them. "But it's really not necessary."

"It is for me," she said, stopping at the stairs, but not turning around. She didn't want to look at him. "I really need to, Daniel. I know you'd rather I weren't here, but I need to feel that I'm helping. I can't just pretend nothing's wrong and let someone else handle it."

Daniel laughed, a low, dark sound that was hardly heard over the snap of the fire. "Of course you can't. That's my style, isn't it? Not yours. Come back down whenever you like, then. We'll keep the vigil together."

CHAPTER SIX

DANIEL knocked twice, softly, on the door to Lindsay's room. There was no answer, but she had pulled the door only half shut, as though she had wanted to be able to hear if anyone called her, so he nudged it with his shoulder until it was wide enough for him to see in.

The fire in the room had died down to a tarnished copper stain on the walls of the hearth, but there was plenty of moonlight. He could easily see the dark flow of Lindsay's hair over the ivory of her pillow. He stood there for a moment, enjoying that cascade of black velvet and mulling over the implications of the half-opened door.

It was, he thought, a very maternal gesture. He knew more about her personal situation now, and he realized that, though she couldn't have been much older than twenty when her parents died, she had obviously taken on the role of parent to her little sister. A good parent, too, he suspected, with the door always cocked, listening for trouble in her sleep. He remembered his own mother doing the same.

But not Jocelyn...oh, no, never Jocelyn. His wife had, on her first night home from the obstetric hospital, firmly shut her bedroom door, leaving the little French au pair and Daniel to answer Alice's cry in the night. He'd never forget the look on the au pair's face when he told her Jocelyn wasn't coming. The young woman's shock had been unmistakable, even by the dim illumination of the nursery night-light.

Standing in the doorway now, he tried for a moment to picture Lindsay sleeping through the thin warble of a baby's hungry cry, Lindsay hiring someone else to bottle feed her newborn daughter. But he couldn't. How could he picture something that was patently impossible?

He leaned against the doorjamb. Strange that he should be so sure—he had learned a lot about Lindsay in these few days of intense intimacy. She couldn't go even four hours, for instance, without calling to check on her little sister. She sang while she cooked, hummed while she tied red satiny Christmas bows. She carried heavy, dirty wood without a complaint and risked her own safety to protect Roc, a man she'd only just met. She sensed Daniel's inner malaise as he sat alone in the dark—and offered to share it. She fussed over Roc's frailty, and she slept with her door ajar.

"Lindsay," he said, but still she didn't rouse. Crossing the room silently, he sat on the edge of the bed. She looked so peaceful, with the moonlight streaming across her serene features, that he hated to wake her. But he knew she'd be desolated if she slept through her "shift."

He twisted one corner of his mouth in a wry half grin. She'd undoubtedly find a way to blame him for the power outage that had silenced her alarm clock. Judging from her comments earlier tonight, Daniel knew she blamed him for everything from global warming to hangnails.

Well, maybe she had a point. Perhaps, by being so strict with his employees, he *had* given his managers the wrong signals. Browder should have known that, given Lindsay's dire circumstances, Daniel wouldn't have declined her request to work from home. And he certainly would never have fired her, even as maddened with worry as he had been that last day, if he had realized how precarious her situation was.

It made him strangely uncomfortable to think back on that. Newly orphaned, locked in a custody battle, out of work and out of money, with Christmas only days away...she must have been wretched.

He shifted, but his discomfort wasn't physical, so the redistribution of his weight didn't help. Luckily, while he had been alone downstairs watching Roc these past few hours, he had come up with a plan to make amends. Now he just had to get her awake and downstairs.

"Lindsay." She was sleeping with one arm crooked over her head, and he touched the tip of her elbow lightly. "Lindsay, wake up."

Her eyes drifted open, and she stared at him a moment in a soft, unfocused confusion. "Daniel?" Then a sharp fear replaced the bemusement. "Daniel!" She clutched his forearms with both hands, her slim fingers tense. "What is it? Is Roc worse?"

"No." He shook his head, cupping her elbows reassuringly with his palms. Her grip loosened a little, though she didn't let go entirely. "He's much better. He was conscious for a little while a couple of hours ago, though he was still fairly dazed. Right now he's sleeping again, but it's a very good sign that he was awake at all."

She let her eyes float shut. "Thank goodness," she said softly. "You frightened me."

The brandy had acted like a sleeping pill, he realized. She was adorably groggy. "I just came up to tell you that it's about three-thirty," he said. "You said you wanted to come down and sit with him awhile. If he wakes up again, I know he'd like to see you there."

She shifted her head on the pillow, looking for her bedside clock. "Three-thirty?" She sounded troubled. "How can it be? I set my alarm." She looked back at him, blinking. "What's wrong with the clock?"

"It's not working. The power went out a little while ago."

Her gaze went immediately to the window. Where once the outdoor floodlights had illuminated the grounds like a white-carpeted showroom, now there was only a muted blue moonglow sifting through the trees. It fell in complicated patterns of blue and black, shadow and light, across the mounded snow.

"Oh," she said, her voice husky, her tone still slightly disoriented. "It's beautiful."

It was. The sky must be very clear, he thought, and the moon very bright. Otherwise nothing at all would have been visible—the house would have seemed to float in an endless dark sea. He scanned the treetops...yes, there it was—the huge poker chip of a moon, a bluish circle with one slightly dented edge, the evergreen branches etched in black upon its surface. It would probably be full by Christmas. A mistletoe moon, as Alice used to call it.

He transferred his gaze back to Lindsay, who was still sleepily mesmerized by the scene, her palms resting lightly on his forearms, as if she had forgotten who he was, where they were...everything except the night sky outside her window.

As he looked down at her, his gut tightened.

The reaction was so instinctive, so unexpected, that it startled him. He had always known she was beautiful, of course. He had seen her come alive by firelight, with the gold dancing across her hair, the amber warming her cheeks. But that had meant nothing, really. He had known dozens of hotly sensual women, from Jocelyn on down to his latest Saturday night theater companion, and he had long ago learned how to enjoy the sizzle without needing to touch the flame.

But this wasn't fire. This was a mysterious crystal purity that knocked the breath right out of him. Moonlight silvered the edges of her tranquil profile, then reached in and painted the hollows of her face with cool blue shadows. The pale sheets, tucked up under her arms, draped her in innocence, but he could just make out the graceful dip and swell of her body beneath the rippling folds.

A tremor of longing ran through him. She reminded him, suddenly, of the angel that once had been placed atop his Christmas tree, all flowing blue satin and shimmering tinsel. Try as he might, he couldn't make the fancy go away. He found himself imagining that, if Lindsay were to rise from this bed right now, she would slowly unfold behind her two trailing wings of graceful, opalescent feathers.

He closed his eyes, squeezed them so hard they hurt, trying to banish the insane image. Angels. Wings. Nonsense. Why would an angel have such a profoundly human effect on his body? And yet, God help him, she did look like an angel, and he wanted her more than he had ever wanted any woman.

He felt his fingers tighten on her arms, and against his will his thumbs began to caress the inside of her elbows. Her skin was cool and silken. He told himself to stop, but his muscles wouldn't cooperate. His palms slid slowly along the slim length of her upper arms. Not far, just an inch or two toward her shoulders, not enough to cross the invisible line between friendly comfort and sexual invitation. But he could feel goose bumps rise under his touch.

She turned her head slowly, and her eyes were wide, the dark blue irises huge and deep. There was a question in those eyes, but she didn't move her arms away. Her fingers, still spread out along his forearms, quivered slightly.

"Daniel," she said, her voice throaty, and this time she didn't sound sleepy.

He didn't answer her. What could he say? It sounded like some scummy singles bar pickup line. *You look like an angel, baby, and I want you to take me to heaven.*

Perhaps no words were necessary. Maybe she felt it, too—this sensual magic that somehow had streamed in with the moonlight—and maybe she knew how poignantly ephemeral it was. Words might make it fly away forever. He felt another slight fluttering of her fingertips, saw her lips soften and part, and he allowed himself to hope.

"We should go down," she said, but the words sounded forced, as if her thoughts and her voice weren't working in sync.

"Should we?" he asked in a low voice.

She took a breath, shuddering as though her lungs were too stiff to let the air in properly. He knew how that felt. His own chest had been tightening painfully for the past ten minutes, until now the tension had spread out into all his limbs.

"Yes." She seemed to be reduced to one-syllable answers, but she kept her dark eyes fixed on his. "Roc."

His hands stilled. She was right, though he didn't want to admit it. They ought to go back downstairs immediately. Roc shouldn't be left alone, in case he awakened again and tried to get up.

As if she sensed his hesitation, she swallowed, ducking her chin with the effort, and summoned up a full sentence. "You see," she said, "I was thinking that, when they come to get him tomorrow, perhaps they could take me, too." She licked her lips, and the moonlight glistened on the moisture she left behind. "Do you think there might be room in the emergency vehicle for me?"

For a moment he didn't breathe, almost angry as he watched the moment slip through his fingers. He had known it would happen. He had known that words, any words, would chase away the delicate magic.

He felt like cursing. Why had she spoken? Her lips, so full and sensual a moment ago, were tightly closed, her face tense and unyielding. Her fingers were dead weights, lifeless against his arms. He looked at his hands, curled white-knuckled against her flesh, and then he slowly let them drop away.

Free of her physical spell, his mind began to clear. How clever of her, he thought, to remind him that she would be fleeing as soon as she possibly could. But why had he needed reminding? What on earth had he been thinking? Lindsay wasn't some Christmas fairy who had floated into his world on the milky beam of a mistletoe moon. She was, instead, a rather angry young businesswoman who had been stranded here by a dangerous snowstorm and could hardly wait for her chance to escape his mountain—and him.

As clearly as if she were still speaking, he heard the eloquent subtext behind her question. The emotional aftermath of Roc's injury, the unfamiliar brandy nightcap, and the unearthly beauty of this silent hour had all conspired to make her momentarily vulnerable, she was telling him. But only momentarily. He needn't think she would fall into her enemy's arms just because she was frightened and lonely and ever-so-slightly tipsy.

"Room for you to go with Roc?" he said crisply, recovering his poise. "Yes, I hope so."

She nodded, a minute movement that indicated none of the relief she must be feeling. He told himself he should be relieved, too. He had come up here with an uneasy spirit, his peace of mind rankled by the accusations she had hurtled at him. He had even formulated a plan to wipe the name of Lindsay Blaisdell off his list of sins forever.

He wanted that. He wanted to be free of any guilt where she was concerned. But if, in some fit of moonlight madness, he made love to her here—well, however transcendent it might be for the moment, the memory of how he had exploited her vulnerability would be an ugly, permanent smear on his conscience.

"Don't worry. I hadn't forgotten how eager you are to leave," he said, working for a normal tone, trying to appreciate his narrow escape. "When I telephoned them about Roc I asked for transport for two. They said they'd do their best."

She nodded again, hugging the sheet to her breast in both fists while watching him from those huge, dark eyes. "Thank you," she said with an absurd formality.

"My pleasure." He tried not to sound sarcastic. He stood up, suddenly realizing the room was terribly cold. He glanced toward the hearth, which was now just a lifeless, soot-blackened hole in the wall. The fire had finally gone out.

"Why don't you get dressed and come on down?" He was already halfway to the door. "It's much warmer by the main fire. I'll wait for you there."

If it hadn't been so cold, she might not have gone downstairs at all, not until the ambulance showed up to take her out of here. But though she layered herself in Doreen's jeans, flannel shirt, turtlenecked sweater and even-fringed leather jacket, the temperature in her room kept falling, until her fingertips hurt, and she could see every breath she took floating in the air in front of her. Finally she gave up and, pulling Doreen's third set of woolen mukluks over her frozen toes, she padded silently down the staircase.

The great room by candlelight was an eerie sight. The fire blazed like a demon's mouth in the center of the room, and at least two dozen tapers flickered in various candlesticks that had been set out around the perimeter.

Daniel looked up from a chess game he seemed to be playing against himself by the bright glow of an eight-armed candelabra. "I was about to mount a search party," he said with a smile that looked mysterious in the shifting light. "Did you lose your way?"

In spite of the Phantom of the Opera set design, she was reassured by his friendly tone. She smiled back politely, glad that he was going to pretend their encounter upstairs hadn't ever happened.

"I wasted half an hour looking for something a little tamer to wear," she said, feathering the beaded fringe of her jacket self-consciously. "I feel as if I'm dressed for a costume party."

"You look fine. You look quite nice, actually," he said, but he was using his most cordial, company tone, and the compliment sounded like something from a script. He looked at her only briefly, then returned his attention to the chessboard.

After that, she just prowled for several minutes, strangely restless. She checked Roc's forehead and adjusted the blanket around his shoulders. She stirred at the fire with one of the brass pokers. Finally, she plucked a magazine from the coffee table and settled herself in the other armchair.

The light from the candelabra was quite bright enough for reading, but she could barely force herself to absorb a single word, alternating between casting worried glances at Roc and watching Daniel over the open pages of the magazine. He seemed almost as unaware of her presence as Roc was, and his sublime indifference began, ironically, to grate on her nerves.

She began to wonder whether she might have entirely imagined the scene upstairs.

What *had* happened up there? Had a spark of pure, electric attraction really ignited between them? Or had it all been her imagination? After all, nothing had been said, nothing had really been done. Going over it detail by detail in her mind, she realized she had actually read the whole sexual byplay in the cloudy blue depths of his eyes—a notoriously unreliable form of communication by any standards.

Oh, good God, wouldn't it have been terrible if she had said something truly stupid? She remembered feeling a fierce, rather primitive, desire for him to kiss her. Suppose she had asked him to? Suppose she had put her arms around his neck and pulled him down to her breast?

The magazine rustled in her unsteady hands as she considered how foolish she would have looked. He would have been shocked, wouldn't he, encountering a bold-as-brass overture from the woman who had told him off royally only hours earlier? She was a little shocked herself.

She peeked over at him. What, she wondered, would have happened? He was, after all, a very normal, red-blooded American male. He might have accepted the invitation anyway, not caring whether it made any logical sense...

The massive fireplace was pulsing out waves of heat, and she was suddenly so warm she had to take off Doreen's jacket. Without it, she felt slightly less ridiculous, though the sweater was loud, too, with big silver and turquoise geometric shapes outlined in sequins. Doreen's self-confidence levels must have been off the charts.

Draping the jacket over the back of her chair, she returned to her magazine, wishing she could work up a consuming interest in the latest senate scandal. But out of the corner of her eye she could see Daniel's hand hovering over a pawn, then tilting it speculatively with one long forefinger. It was inordinately distracting.

Daniel spoke into the silence. "Want to play a game of chess?"

She looked up, surprised.

"I'm getting tired of checkmating myself," he said, arching one brow impudently. "Care to take a turn?"

"A turn getting checkmated?" She put the magazine down in her lap. "What makes you think you could beat me?" she asked. "I'm a pretty mean chess player."

He chuckled as he began to rearrange the pieces, obviously taking her acquiescence for granted. "I don't believe you're a pretty mean anything, Lindsay," he said. "Remember, we've been negotiating this Hamilton Homes deal, you and I—and I happen to know that you don't have an ounce of killer instinct."

"That's different," she said, reaching over to arrange her side. "Hamilton Homes represents real people, real lives. Believe me, when it's just a game, I'm perfectly content to go for the throat."

"All right, then," he said, easing the chessboard toward her. "Prove it."

If it was designed as a dare, it worked. She immediately determined to win, no matter what it took. She contemplated the board for a moment. Up close, the set was even more beautiful and detailed than she had realized. Armored knights rode rearing horses; queens wore flowing gowns and coronets. Even the rooks were real castles with carved-stone walls. She'd never seen anything like it.

She moved her queen's pawn forward two squares with a bit of a flourish.

"A conservative opener," he said, moving a pawn of his own face-to-face with hers. "Who taught you to play?"

"My father," she said, studying the board some more, struggling to remember one of those particularly tricky maneuvers her father had always been trying out. Ah, yes... that might do... She moved her queen diagonally three squares, praying that she had remembered one of the tricks that actually worked. Unfortunately, most of them hadn't. Her father had usually been very drunk and very reckless.

"I hope he was good," Daniel said. After a couple of minutes he surprised her by moving his knight pawn out two spaces. "Roc taught me. He's unbeatable."

She glanced up briefly. "Really? Roc? Chess seems rather tame for Roc."

Daniel grinned. "Yeah, well, I think he was looking for something to keep me off the streets. I was about twelve at the time. My friends and I had just discovered that cherished male pastime—rearranging each other's faces with our fists."

She chuckled, but she didn't take her eyes off the chessboard, her thoughts racing through the various options for her next move.

"Ugh," she said. "Sounds painful."

"Strangely enough, it wasn't," he said. "I guess twelve-year-old boys aren't particularly sensitive."

She looked up, smiling. The candlelight danced in his blue eyes, and one corner of his mouth was suspiciously twisted.

"That's certainly what Christy tells me," she said. Her hand hovered over her bishop, but she hesitated. Something here didn't look right—was it possible that only one pawn stood between her queen and his king?

He didn't seem to notice his jeopardy. In fact, he didn't seem to be thinking about the game at all. He leaned back in his chair and stretched.

"Anyhow, I remember Roc said I'd better learn to use my brain instead of my brawn," he went on, "since clearly I was going to be puny."

Puny... Lindsay couldn't help herself: she let her gaze sweep across the broad expanse of his shoulders, the long stretch of his muscular thigh.

"Oh, yes, clearly," she echoed wryly. "A runt."

He leaned forward again, and they both studied the board for several long minutes without speaking. She tried to sit perfectly still, not betraying by even a twitch of her fingers how close she was to checkmating his king.

It would be great fun to beat Daniel at this chess game, and she somehow sensed he wouldn't really mind very much if she did. His ego was robust enough to withstand it. And why shouldn't it be? It was undoubtedly fed well and regularly with much meatier dishes than this.

Nonetheless, his new, light mood was charming...and contagious, as he obviously intended it to be.

Bravely she moved her bishop.

"Interesting..." His fingers floated over a pawn, then switched to a knight. But before he moved either piece, he looked up abruptly, the candlelight still dancing in his eyes.

"You know what? I think you're right, Lindsay—this game is too tame. We'll go to sleep at this rate, and the fire will go out, and they'll find us here in the morning, frozen into little ice statue copies of The Thinker." He waggled his eyebrows in a terrific imitation of Roc at his most mischievous. "What say we do a little something to heat things up? Something to make it more interesting?''

"Well," she said, tilting her head and smiling, "if you're thinking about Strip Chess, I should warn you I'm wearing one sweater, two undershirts, and three pairs of mukluks."

He ducked his head to check her feet. "Darn that Doreen," he said in mock disappointment. "She always was overdressed."

Straightening, he eyed her speculatively, running his thumb and forefinger idly down the carved sides of his rook's tower. "Seriously, though," he said. "I was really thinking we might bet something on this game."

She pulled her gaze from his fingers, though the motion was mesmerizing. "Like what?"

"Like Hamilton Homes."

Flushing deeply, she met his eyes. "Is that a joke? It's not very funny."

"No joke." He still stroked the rook. "I'm quite serious. If you win, Robert gets to keep Hamilton Homes."

"Also not funny." She tightened her lips, intensely disappointed that Daniel would toy with her this way. They had been having such a pleasant time—she had even begun to believe they might be...well, if not friends, then at least not enemies. "Robert doesn't *want* to keep Hamilton Homes, remember? He can't afford it."

"He'll be able to afford it when I tell him what I know about that development."

"What exactly does that mean?" Her voice was skeptical. "What could you possibly know that Robert doesn't already know? It's his development, remember?"

Finally Daniel let go of the rook. "Come on, Lindsay...think about it rationally. You don't believe I'm buying Robert's company out of the goodness of my heart, do you?'' He registered her incredulous expression and smiled dryly. ''Of course you don't. You know I must have something up my sleeve, some information that even your beloved Robert doesn't have—''

''He's not my beloved Robert,'' she broke in heatedly. She knew that wasn't the point, but she didn't like Daniel's sarcastic tone. Besides, it seemed important, somehow, that he understand that Robert was not her boyfriend. He was just her friend. And her boss.

''I'm glad to hear it.'' He raised one eyebrow in that arrogant way she was beginning to recognize. It was annoying as blazes, but it was devastatingly attractive at the same time. ''Anyhow, I do have some information about the development, Lindsay. You can count on that. If I tell Robert what I know, he'll have no trouble getting a loan to tide him over until his luck changes.''

She hesitated. Smiling, he swept his hand over the board. ''So what do you say, white queen? All the computers, fax machines and high-tech bells and whistles have been silenced, at least for tonight. It's come down to just you and me and this chessboard. If you win, I tell Robert my secret.''

Her insides were warring against themselves. She tried to clamp down on the commotion so that she could think clearly. ''And if *you* win?'' she asked.

''Then I get Hamilton Homes,'' he said. His brow arched even higher. ''And I get you along with it.''

CHAPTER SEVEN

HE COULD tell that she was almost too stunned to speak.

"Me?" A dark stain spread over her cheekbones. "You can't be serious."

"But I am." He watched as both indignation and incredulity washed across her face, the emotions bumping into one another as they fought for dominance. "Why should that surprise you? You work for Hamilton Homes, which I am proposing to buy. Therefore, doesn't it logically follow that you will work for me?"

"Oh," she said, her flush deepening. "I thought you meant . . ."

He smiled. "Something more personal?"

Indignation obviously had risen to the top of her emotional pileup. Her spine straightened, and her eyes narrowed.

"Yes, actually, that *is* what I thought," she said stiffly, staring him down with those angry—but still beautiful— eyes. "Ridiculous, perhaps, but frankly, I find your interpretation equally absurd. You can't honestly believe that I'd come back to work for you, can you? Any more than I can believe you'd want me to."

"Why not?" He kept his smile in place. "You're going to need a job, aren't you? You haven't suddenly become independently wealthy?"

She sat up even straighter, though he wouldn't have thought it was possible. "No, but Robert has asked me to stay on." Her chin was lifted so high he wondered how she could even see him. "As his personal assistant."

Oh, he had, had he? Daniel picked up the nearest chess piece and turned it end over end through his fingers, trying to work off some of the irrational tension he felt at her announcement. Such a generous display of loyalty for a man on the brink of bankruptcy! Robert Hamilton didn't miss a trick, did he? Before he was through proving what a saint he was, Lindsay would be so grateful she'd probably imagine she was in love with the man.

"I see," he said. The sarcasm in his voice was blatant, but he didn't much care anymore. "How good of him. Tell me, though...what exactly *are* the duties of a personal assistant to a man who no longer has any personal business?"

Her eyes were narrowed so tightly even the candlelight couldn't reach them. "I don't think I understand what you mean—"

"Oh, yes, you do." As if watching himself from some remote emotional distance, Daniel wondered why he was being such an ass. Lindsay's personal relationship with her employer wasn't really any of his business. He was well aware of that. But he didn't seem to be able to stop himself. "I mean that, in return for his excessive loyalty, Robert Hamilton may want more than just your gratitude."

It was way over the line, and he knew it. He fully expected her to open fire, to tell him what a nasty-minded, meddling bastard he was, how he wasn't fit to utter the saintly Robert Hamilton's name...

Instead, to his amazement, her chin lowered slowly, and little by little her tense, narrowed eyes relaxed into their normal, charming almond shape. Sighing, she dug one hand into her hair and rubbed her temple with the heel of her palm.

"You're right," she said wearily. "He does want more. But he knows he's not going to get it. I've explained to him that I don't love him, at least not that way. He's a very special friend, but I've made it clear there will never be more than that between us." She frowned. "It's just that—he doesn't want to accept it."

He nodded. "I can imagine," he said, feeling his first spurt of pity for the other man. "But have you considered that maybe you're not doing him any favors by staying on with him? At the very least it's got to be hard to see you every day and know he can't have you. Even worse, it may be keeping his hopes alive on some kind of artificial life support."

She put her elbow on the table, resting her cheek in her hand. "I know," she said dully. "I know. I've pretty much decided the same thing myself. That's why I'm not really going to keep working for him after the sale goes through. I just told you that because—" She looked down at the chessboard. "I don't know why I said it. I've been interviewing with other companies for weeks now, and one of them has offered me a job. I'm planning to leave just as soon as this deal is completed."

She looked up again, and her eyes were like blue fire in the lambent candlelight. "I would have told him the other day, but then he got sick and had to be rushed into surgery. Somehow that didn't seem like the right time to hand him my resignation."

She looked at him earnestly, as if she really wanted him to understand. "I honestly do feel that I owe him something, Daniel. He helped me through a couple of very tough years. I was hoping to bring home an agreement on this sale before I had to give him the bad news."

Daniel had to fight the urge to reach out and touch her tired face. She was such a crazy idealist, wasn't she? He felt a sudden surge of relief that he had decided to buy Hamilton's damn company. If he had said no, he could almost imagine Lindsay marrying the man just to console him. His whole body tensed at the thought. Hamilton wouldn't be ashamed to play Lindsay's sympathies for all they were worth. Play them all the way to the altar, if he could.

But that wasn't going to happen. Not if Daniel could help it.

"Then take my bet, Lindsay," he said. "Let's finish this game. If you win, you can bring Hamilton back something even better than a contract. You can bring him a second chance."

She started to shake her head, but he stopped her by shoving his pawn forward two spaces. "Play," he ordered. "You owe him, remember? How will you live with your conscience if you deny him this opportunity to hang on to his dream?"

She obviously knew she was beaten. She didn't even bother to argue. She just lowered her gaze to the chessboard and made a rather reckless move with her king's knight. Daniel held back a smile, but he was immensely relieved. By tomorrow both their consciences would be feeling much better.

It took him almost two hours to do it without arousing her suspicions, but he finally lost. Her queen found his king, backed him deep into a corner, and it was over.

"Checkmate," she said in a near whisper. She looked up, apparently too stunned or too tired—or both—to feel much of anything, much less the elation he had expected.

Without a word he stood up, walked over to the desk and found the fax he'd received two nights ago. The news of the corporate relocations was outlined in detail there. Even a businessman as lousy as Robert Hamilton could surely parlay those facts into an extension on his loans.

He handed the paper to her without a word, and she stared at it, her eyes fixed and clearly unable to read. At that moment the telephone rang.

He grabbed it, growling roughly. "Hello?"

He listened to the short message, then turned to Lindsay, who was still staring blankly at the faxed report. "Seems all the luck is on your side today," he said. "That was my pilot. The winds are down—they're low enough for him to fly. He'll be here to get Roc in about two hours."

She turned toward him slowly. It showed the measure of her numb torpor, he thought, that she didn't even smile at this long-awaited, desperately prayed-for news.

"The helicopter?" She sounded only half aware of what she was saying. "Does that mean that I—?"

"He has room for two passengers, Lindsay," Daniel said shortly. "It means you're going home."

It didn't take her long to get ready. She folded all of Doreen's outrageous clothes back into the box, donned her own full, gray skirt and white sweater. Then she called Christy. Lastly she gathered her briefcase full of Hamilton Homes papers, including the amazing fax that just might be the miracle Robert had been praying for.

All that done, she still had about an hour to wait, and she wandered downstairs to sit beside Roc for a while. She hoped that Daniel might join her, but he was conspicuously absent. Curiously deflated, she stared at the chess set, where the king still stood in checkmate.

After the call from the pilot, she and Daniel had discussed the fax and its implications for a very few minutes. He had assured her that, if Robert couldn't negotiate another extension on his payments, Daniel's own company would be glad to offer a loan to Hamilton

Homes. Either way, he said, Robert should be able to keep his precious development, and his company.

It had all seemed rather like a dream to Lindsay, and she had an uncomfortable feeling now that she hadn't asked any of the right questions. But she had had so little time, and Daniel had seemed so remote, keeping things strictly business, acting as if playing a chess match for control of a company were something he did every day.

After filling her in on the basic details, Daniel had received another call, and another one after that. And then another. She began to wish the phone lines had gone out with the electricity. Clearly his business day had begun, complete with a workaholic's chain-telephoning. The strange, intimate little interlude they'd shared in the night, with its silly laughter and curious honesty, was over.

Finally, with sign-language gestures, she'd excused herself, letting him know she'd be upstairs getting ready. He had nodded absently, scribbling on a notepad while he talked, hardly aware of her departure. She hadn't seen him since.

"Well, hi there, angel."

Lindsay could hardly believe her ears. It was Roc. She jumped from her chair and rushed to the side of the sofa. She felt a surge of happiness just to see the older man's eyes open, twinkling at her with only slightly less mischief than they'd possessed before his accident.

"Hello, there," she said, her throat thick with emotion. "It certainly is good to see you awake!" She touched his forehead. "How are you feeling?"

He scowled. "I feel like road kill." He tried to sit up, but he didn't get far. Lindsay suspected that it was his pain as much as her restraining hand that forced him back down. "What the hell happened to my head?"

"You were up on the roof," she said calmly, pulling his hand away from the bandaged spot. "Daniel says you slipped and hit your head on the chimney."

"Slipped? He said that?" Roc huffed emphatically. "Well, excuse me, but Roc Richter doesn't just *slip*, like Charlie goddamn Chaplin, thank you very much." He scowled. "Something must have tripped me."

"Tripped?" Daniel appeared at the kitchen door. He must have been in there the whole time, Lindsay thought. He just hadn't cared to come out until he heard Roc's voice. "On what? Maybe an old banana peel? We have a big problem with people throwing their trash up on top of the roof in the middle of a blizzard."

Though he couldn't see Daniel over the back of the sofa, Roc rolled his eyes for Lindsay's benefit. "Sarcastic son of a sailor, isn't he? Thinks he's cute, no doubt." He raised his voice. "I probably tripped over one of your big clumsy feet, Danny Boy. But if you'll bring me an aspirin for this head I might not sue you."

Apparently Daniel had already thought of that. He came around the edge of the sofa, glass in one hand, aspirin bottle in the other. "I want that in writing," he said.

Roc reached out for the aspirin. "I'll tattoo it on your forehead if you like. Now give me the damn pills, will you? Somebody's playing the bongos on my brain."

Lindsay held the glass of water, while Daniel stood behind Roc, propping him up just enough to swallow safely. It frightened her to see how Roc's face paled when he tried to move. He cursed intensely, using a couple of words Lindsay hadn't ever heard before. The pain must be terrible, she thought, glancing nervously up at Daniel. He was frowning, and his eyes were dark, his brows knitted tightly.

But when Daniel spoke again, his voice revealed nothing of the worry she'd glimpsed in his eyes.

"Charming language," he said mildly, coming around and sitting on the edge of the coffee table. "It'll be a relief to turn you over to the doctors, you know that? Maybe they can sterilize your mouth while they're sewing up your head."

Reaching over, he took one corner of the bandage between his thumb and forefinger and began, very slowly, to lift it. Lindsay was amazed at the contrast between his rough, teasing tone and the infinite gentleness of his hands.

"The helicopter should be here in a few minutes," he added, bending closer to look at the gash. "Until then, try to remember there's a lady present, will you please?"

"Helicopter?" Roc knocked Daniel's hand away irritably. "Stop that. It hurts. What's the damn helicopter for?"

Daniel returned to his ministrations just as if there had been no interruption. "For you, you old fool." He patted the bandage back in place. "You've knocked a hole in your head. If you had any brains, they'd have fallen out by now."

"What, this little thing?" Roc tapped the bandage with his forefinger airily, which would have been more effective if he hadn't winced. "Don't you think you're making a monster out of a minnow here, Danny Boy? Calling in the marines over this scratch?"

"I think I'm making a sensible decision," Daniel said matter-of-factly. "You've been unconscious for nearly twelve hours, you know. Like it or not, you're taking the helicopter out of here today. God knows when we might see another one."

"Sorry. No can do." Roc put his weight on his elbows and struggled up to a half-sitting position. "Miss Lindsay and I have a date for Christmas dinner."

"Well, you'll have to celebrate back in Phoenix." Daniel didn't look at Lindsay. "She's going with you."

Roc's face fell. "She is?"

Lindsay poked at his knee lightly. "Gosh," she said with a mock pout. "That's a flattering reaction! Couldn't you at least pretend to be happy about it?"

"No." Roc looked stubborn. "I couldn't."

Daniel glanced over at her briefly, then faced Roc again. "You knew she needed to get home as soon as possible, Roc. Her sister's waiting for her." He sounded serious for the first time. "You knew that," he repeated.

"Yeah, but..." Suddenly Roc didn't look irritable anymore. He looked exhausted, as if even this short conversation had been too taxing. He dropped his head against the armrest wearily. "But I—"

"But nothing." Daniel's voice firmed. "It's settled. Landwer will be here any minute." He patted the older man's shoulder, leaving his hand there protectively. "It's going to be fine, Roc. Lindsay will take care of you for me."

Without speaking, Roc put his weathered hand over Daniel's. Lindsay felt a lump in her throat as she looked at the two hands, one youthful and tanned, the other gnarled and spotted with age, but both strong, masculine...and apparently capable of great tenderness. She felt that there was some unspoken message passing between the two men. She wondered whether she ought to leave the room. Perhaps if she were not there they could speak more freely.

"Danny, it's just that I don't want you to be alone." Roc's voice was altered by emotion, a sound Lindsay had never heard before. "Damn it, you stubborn dunderhead. It's Christmas, and you need somebody to—"

"I'll spend the whole day on the phone, Roc. Or going over those Middleton contracts. You know how it always is."

"Yeah, I know," Roc said, and his voice was trembling. Lindsay averted her gaze, feeling more in the way than ever. "But whatever you manage to busy yourself with on Christmas Day, I've always been here. You've never been really alone."

"Roc, listen to me. It's just another day. I will be fine." Daniel spoke slowly, enunciating each word carefully through a clenched jaw. Even Lindsay could hear that Roc was pushing the issue too far.

She stood up, brushing imaginary dust from her skirt. "I think I'll wait out on the porch for the helicopter," she said, striving for a nonchalant tone. "I haven't seen much of the scenery, and I want to be able to tell Christy all about it when I get back."

They didn't try to stop her. With a smile for Roc, she grabbed her coat, slipped it on and, easing the front door open, stepped out onto the porch.

Breathing deeply in the cold, fresh air, she leaned against the railing. Though she had merely been inventing an excuse to leave the men alone, the sight that greeted her was well worth seeing. The sky was a cloudless, pure Italian blue. Near the lodge, where the grounds had been cleared, unfiltered sunlight glistened on the snow, making the windblown mounds twinkle like dazzling heaps of abandoned diamonds.

Farther down, where the ground began to slope away, majestic ponderosa pines, blue spruce and Douglas firs wore soft, thick coats of snow, like ice cream confections dipped in velvety white chocolate.

Looking at all that luminous beauty, she wondered why she didn't feel more excited. It was the kind of day that seemed to promise all your wishes would come true. Many of them already had. Roc was awake and, though weak, seemed destined to a full recovery. Robert would be able to keep Hamilton Homes. And somewhere nearby, just over the tops of those towering trees, a pilot was headed this way, coming to set her free. Christy had sounded so happy to hear that she was coming home.

And yet a small, dense lump of sorrow lay at the bottom of Lindsay's psyche. She wanted to go home. Of course she did. Who wouldn't want to be home for Christmas? Still—somehow the thought of leaving made her sad. She hated the image of all those red bows lying unnoticed in the wicker basket, never to be strung along the banister as she and Roc had planned. She hated knowing that the albums of Christmas carols would be returned to the dusty cabinet, silenced for another three years . . . or more.

The telephone began to ring inside, its tinny buzz just barely audible. Most of all, she realized, she hated the thought of Daniel here alone, in this eerie, quiet, frozen world, with only his business calls to keep him company. It was physically painful to think what awful memories he must nurse when he sat alone in the cold blue darkness. He would never tell her now. She would never see him again.

She heard a sound at the door, and she turned around, brushing moisture from her eyes before it could turn to ice on her lashes. It was Daniel. His face was grim.

"Oh, God," she said, instinctively fearing the worst. "Is Roc all right?"

"He's fine." Daniel touched her elbow reassuringly. "You saw him. It'll take more than a bash on the head to stop that man."

Her heart slowed down slightly, but Daniel's small smile somehow wasn't completely convincing. Something was wrong, even if it wasn't Roc. She wondered...that last telephone call... Perhaps it had been bad news. "Is it Landwer? Is it that the helicopter can't get here after all?"

"No. He's coming." Daniel stepped beyond her, out onto the porch, zipping his jacket and flipping up the collar to protect his neck against the freezing air. His dark hair curled around the upturned bit of heather-gray fleece as he turned his head away from her, scanning the trees below them.

"What, then?" She put her hand on his arm, unable to bear the anxiety. Her nerves were already strung too tightly. "Tell me, Daniel. I know something is wrong. I can see it on your face."

He turned toward her. His eyes were as intensely blue as the sky. His brows, startlingly dark above them were knitted against the uncomfortably bright sunlight.

"When Landwer fueled up in Denver, the highway patrol told him about another emergency. It's Mrs. Patterson. She lives on the south face, about a mile below us." He put his hand over hers gently. The gesture reminded her of the way Roc had touched Daniel's hand earlier—and she knew that the news was bad indeed. That gesture held a world of pity in it.

She waited for him to tell the rest, her breath shallow, misting in the air between them.

"She's seventy-five years old. Lives alone." His hand tightened. "Her family's worried sick about her. She hasn't been well lately, and now that the power's out—"

Lindsay began shaking her head. "There must be another helicopter," she said, though she knew it wasn't true. Why else would Daniel be out here, with that pity in his eyes? "There must be someone else who could take her down..."

"Not today." Daniel's voice was gentle, but definite. "There are dozens of other emergencies, most of them much worse than hers."

"What about a car? A Jeep? A snowmobile?"

"The Littledale bridge is out," Daniel said, closing the door on her desperate hopes with one quiet sentence. "No one can drive onto or off this mountain until it's repaired. That could be days."

Though her heart still pounded its desperation, she was out of suggestions. She just stared at him, mutely asking for a miracle.

"It's up to you, Lindsay," he said softly. "I can have Landwer check on her on the way out. But there's not room for another person in a chopper that size. And there isn't time for two trips. The wind is already picking up."

She made a small, unhappy sound, and he touched her chin. "I mean it, Lindsay. It's your decision. If you say you still want to go, you'll go."

In the near distance she heard the soft putter of a helicopter's rotor blades as they sliced through the frigid air. The sound grew louder, until finally she could see the speck sliding across the sky like a big black marble.

Then suddenly the whole scene splintered into a haze of rainbowed prisms as weak tears collected in her eyes. She blinked them back furiously, ashamed.

"Of course Mrs. Patterson must have my place. Will you tell Landwer? I'll go in and explain to Roc." She turned away slowly. "And then I'll call my sister. I know she'll understand."

Daniel wasn't nearly as sure as Lindsay seemed to be that Christy was going to be particularly understanding.

The kid would probably wonder why an old lady's needs should take precedence over her own, and he didn't doubt that she'd say so. Loudly. With sound effects. Frankly, the twelve-year-old's humanitarian instincts didn't seem to be all that highly developed.

With Lindsay as her role model, though, he had to assume that they someday would be.

Lindsay had been utterly poised throughout the difficult scene of forcing a bellowing Roc into the helicopter and saying a poignant goodbye. Landwer, ordinarily a rather tough old nut, had been so moved that he had offered to risk a return trip, ice storm or no ice storm, but Lindsay had gracefully thanked him and declined.

Never once, after she got her initial shock in check, had she given any hint of her own disappointment. Daniel was impressed.

Still, he imagined that her call to Christy might prove rather unpleasant, complete with tears and raging at the Phoenix end. It was with hopes of lending moral support that he wandered up to her room a little while later, when he saw the green light blink on his office telephone, signifying that the extension was in use.

"Yes, Gran, I do understand that she's outside right now," Lindsay was saying. Her voice was strained. "No, I don't think it can wait until she comes in for lunch. The sooner she knows the truth, the sooner she can start dealing with it."

He stopped in the doorway, wondering whether he could be hearing right. The grandmother didn't want to call Christy to the telephone?

Seeing him there, Lindsay smiled weakly and shrugged, indicating her helplessness to persuade the woman on the other end of the line. "Gran, please. Please go get her. I really think she needs to know right away." She took a deep breath, her knuckles white around the telephone cord. "Yes, I understand that you'd have to go outside. And that it's raining. I understand that, Gran..."

Something snapped inside him—he couldn't stand to listen to Lindsay practically beg the old woman for a chance to talk to her little sister. What an old bat this "Gran" person must be. He shoved into the room, his arm outstretched.

"Let me talk to her," he said.

Lindsay looked confused, then held out the telephone slowly. He could still hear the old bat jabbering away on the other end. "Your paternal grandmother?" he asked Lindsay, his hand over the mouthpiece. She nodded.

He lifted the phone. "Hello, Mrs. Blaisdell. This is Daniel McKinley," he said politely, though he felt like reaching through the phone and wringing her selfish neck. "How are you? Lindsay says you're having rotten weather in Phoenix today."

Immediately defensive, the woman began hurtling explanations: Christy was outside, feeding a vacationing neighbor's cat; she would have to go out to fetch her; it was raining; she wasn't well; she was a busy woman.

Daniel had no patience for it. After the roller-coaster morning she'd had, Lindsay didn't need this nonsense. But a lifetime of business dealings had taught him when to use force and when to use grease.

So he sympathized, murmuring at appropriate intervals. He even listened to the half-hidden criticisms of Lindsay without losing his temper. Out of the corner of his eye, he saw Lindsay's bewildered expression. He winked at her.

Finally, he figured the situation was sufficiently oiled.

"I'm sure you see our problem, though," he said. "We've already lost our electricity. The phone lines could go down any minute. It could be days before we can get through again. So we really must talk to Christy now." He gave Lindsay a thumbs-up. "Thank you, Mrs. Blaisdell. We'll hold the line."

With a smile, he handed the receiver to Lindsay. "The next voice you hear should be your sister's," he said smugly.

She folded the handset up against her chest. "My God," she whispered. "How did you do it?"

"Easy." He grinned. "I had the foresight to be a male. That kind of bossy old gal is often a chauvinist at heart. Doesn't mind bullying another female, but wouldn't dare try it with a man."

She shook her head wonderingly. "I never thought of it, but actually you may be right."

"Of course I am. You're not the only one with a couple of bats in the family belfry, you know."

She smiled, but just then, apparently hearing some new sound, she jerked the telephone to her ear.

"Christy?" Her voice was anxious, and the smile he'd been so proud of faded from her lips. "Christy, honey, I'm afraid I've got bad news..."

Oh, God. He could hardly bear to listen to this conversation, either. Christy was reacting with predictable fussing and whining, and within minutes Lindsay was practically in tears again.

To avoid the urge to grab the phone away yet another time—it wouldn't do to make a habit of these caveman tactics—he prowled into the hall. But he didn't go far—he stayed within earshot, in case things escalated, in case she needed his help.

For pity's sake, he thought, when had he turned into such a jellyfish? Daniel, who had only three days ago said he prided himself on facing difficult truths, now found that he hated the thought of Lindsay feeling any distress at all.

He must be losing his mind. He suddenly wished desperately that he had never told her about Mrs. Patterson, that he had just put her on that helicopter and sent her away. She would be halfway to Phoenix by now, not here in his guest room, holding back tears, exerting such an inexplicable influence on him . . .

Suddenly there was silence. He walked to the doorway and looked in. Lindsay stood with her back to him, facing the window, her hand still resting on the receiver, which she had already returned to its cradle.

He watched her for a minute. Her breathing was erratic—first deep, with a peculiar hitch in it, then seeming briefly to stop altogether. Her shoulders were held at an unnatural angle, as though she were a marionette whose strings were being yanked too tightly.

He ought to walk away. He told himself to walk away. But he found himself entering the room.

CHAPTER EIGHT

"ARE you all right?" he asked.

Without turning around, she shook her head. The gesture had *leave me alone* written all over it. A wise man would have obeyed. A wise man would have let her cry in peace.

But Daniel moved closer, farther into the room, until he was only a foot or two behind her. "Lindsay, I promise you Christy will be okay. She'll survive, and when you finally do get to celebrate Christmas it will seem twice as special."

"You just don't understand," she said, her voice muffled with tears, but ringing with tension. "You don't know what Christy's been through."

"Tell me."

She drew in a shuddering breath. For a moment he thought she was going to refuse, but suddenly she began to speak.

"My mother died of cancer three years ago," she said, "and after that my father's heart just seemed to break. He drank himself to death within a few months. We couldn't stop him. I couldn't stop him. Christy—" She stopped, took another hitching breath and went on. "Christy found him. I was out on a date...it was the first time in months I hadn't stayed home to sit with him. Christy was there, but she was only nine. She...she came down and..."

She stopped. Her shoulders were shaking. Reaching out without thinking, Daniel put his palms against the trembling. "Shh..."

"But I should have been there," she said, her voice so thick it was almost unrecognizable. "I should be there now."

"It's not your fault," he said. He moved forward and pressed her back against him, absorbing her small, quivering shudders into his own body. "It's not your fault."

He didn't know whether he was talking about her father's death or the blizzard. Or both. But she didn't seem to need an explanation. The bracing warmth of his body seemed to be enough. The shivering subsided slowly, and after a couple of minutes she twisted in his arms, turning to face him. Her deep blue eyes were shimmering with tears, and her cheeks were a maze of shining, wet tracks.

"I'm all right now," she said, trying to smile. "I'm sorry to be such a crybaby. It's just that I know she needs me."

He brushed teardrops from her jawline. "I know," he said. "But it isn't just Christy who's hurting. You need her right now just as much as she needs you."

"Me?" Looking surprised, she shook her head emphatically. "No, no, really. I'm fine."

He held her gaze. "No, you're not. How could you be? Christy isn't the only one who lost her family, you know. You were orphaned that day, too."

"But I was so much older," she protested, trying to dismiss his sympathy, clearly uncomfortable with the concept of needing anything herself. "I understood better—"

"No one ever really understands death." He let his thumbs glide over her cheeks, smoothing away the wetness. "It's painful to lose someone you love, no matter how old you are."

She opened her mouth to deny it, but he put his finger over her lips, blocking the stoic words. It was time to stop being the rock everyone else leaned on. It was taking too much out of her. It was time for someone to worry about Lindsay for a change. She certainly had earned it.

He moved his thumbs up to dry the tears that had pooled under her eyes, and, as he did, she let her lids fall shut slowly. Her lashes sparkled with moisture, and he brushed them softly, too.

"Poor Lindsay. And now here you are, stranded at Christmas in a strange house, on a lonely mountain, with no heat, no light, no friends...locked away with only a man you've hated for years..."

Her eyes drifted open. "I don't hate you," she said with a soft bemusement, as if it surprised her to realize it. "Not anymore."

"I'm glad to hear it." He smoothed her hair back from her face. It was damp, too, but so silky under his fingers that he was tempted to slide his fingers in and bury his hands up to his wrists. Somehow he managed to control the urge.

"That helps a little, I guess," he said, picking one last stray strand from her moist cheek and tucking it behind her ear. "But still, it's hardly the kind of happy family Christmas you were planning, is it? No presents, no turkey, no tree..."

She lifted the corners of her mouth—not quite enough to qualify as a smile, but close enough to make Daniel's heart feel suddenly lighter.

"Well, I do have about a million big red bows," she said. Both teasing and tears lurked beneath the light joke.

God, she was strong, wasn't she? And beautiful. Leaning down, he placed a kiss at the dimpled corner of that brave, trembling mouth. The light touch, which he had meant as a tribute to her courage, sent a jolting electric shock through his system. Caught in the current, he couldn't pull away, though he ordered himself to do so immediately.

Instead, when she didn't protest, his disobedient lips lightly traced the outline of her entire mouth, from edge to edge, lingering at the sensual pout at the center. Her flesh was so sweet, swollen and warm from the emotional storm through which she had just passed. His whole body tightened, wanting more. Wanting it all.

"Daniel…" She looked up at him. Her eyes were wide, and in them he saw the reflection of the same questions that careened through his own mind. What in God's name was he doing? Why had he kissed her like that? What did he want from her?

He didn't have any answers to those questions. Not any good ones.

He tried to tell himself the kiss was just a kind of comfort, offered to soothe her troubled spirit, to show his support and admiration.

But he knew it was a lie. He might not know what it was, but he sure as hell knew what it *wasn't*, and it wasn't by any stretch of the imagination a charity kiss.

"So," he said, lifting his head, retreating into a studied cheer, though it sounded patently false, like a bad bedside manner. "Maybe before the ice storm hits us I can get out there and hunt down some of those items of Christmas joy that we seem to be missing."

Though her lips were still temptingly pink and full, she cooperated by stepping back slightly and smiling politely. "Good heavens," she said. "This sounds serious. Are you going to get out your trusty musket and shoot us a Christmas turkey?"

"Nope." He grinned. "I wouldn't know what to do with the damn thing if I did. Turkey feathers are Roc's department." He lifted one brow. "Unless of course *you*—"

"Not a chance," she said firmly.

"Okay, then. We'll have to settle for the traditional McKinley Christmas dinner. Red omelet with green cornbread stuffing."

"Horrible." Lindsay wrinkled her nose. "I don't think I'll be hungry that day."

Daniel smiled. "Wimp-guts."

She smiled back, and impulsively he grabbed her hand, pulling her to the other side of the room. "Quick," he said. "Come with me. We're going to go somewhere, and you need a whole new costume."

"Where?" He didn't answer, holding on to her hand tightly as he found the box full of Doreen's clothes. He was suddenly, sophomorically excited by the prospect of doing something he hadn't done in years—probably not since he was Christy's age.

"Where?" She stood patiently while he rummaged through the box, looking for the items he needed. After a couple of minutes, though, her patience ran out. Grabbing his hand and staying it, she began to laugh. "Tell me, darn it. Where are we going?"

"Hunting," he said, triumphantly holding up a full set of bright yellow ski clothes. "We're going out to hunt the wild North American Christmas tree."

By the time Lindsay had suited up for the tree hunt, she was exhausted. Never had she donned so many layers at once. Thermal underwear, spandex tights, a long-sleeved tunic that fit like a second skin, a fleecy parka, socks, oversocks, boots, gloves and a ski cap to match. It took half an hour just to get it all put on.

As might have been predicted, every stitch of Doreen's preposterous costume was a neon yellow that made her look, she thought, like a glow-in-the-dark banana.

She presented herself to Daniel, who was waiting in the utility shed, with a sheepish grin. "Good thing there's nobody left on this mountain but us," she said, tucking her hair up into the yellow knitted blob on her head. "I'd hate to be seen in this getup."

Maddeningly, he looked quite marvelous in his own outfit. He had chosen all black, which made him seem daring and dangerous rather than ludicrous and loud, and he hadn't gone for the stretchy spandex look. His pants were made of fleece, and they must have been tapered by a London tailor. They fit so well they hugged his hips, then slid down his legs like black velvet, outlining the bulge of his calves just before they tucked neatly into his boots.

He scanned her from cap to boot. "In about five minutes, you're going to decide you love that outfit. Don't let the color fool you—those are first-rate ski clothes. Doreen knew quality, and she always insisted on having the best."

Not always, Lindsay thought. After all, when Doreen had failed to snare Daniel, she had settled for a "crazy old rich man" named Barnes. The Cheyenne Queen had undoubtedly bought second-best that time.

Daniel pulled on a cap that was almost exactly the shame shade of black as his hair, leveraged his ax out of the stump, and pushed open the shed door with his shoulder.

"Here we go," he said. "Stay close behind me."

She didn't need to be told twice. Once they got outside, she was almost blinded by the sun glinting off the snow, and everything looked so blank that she would have had no idea which way to go. He walked slowly, surefooted but cautious, and she literally followed in his footsteps, as if they were crossing a field of land mines.

They headed up the mountain, where a hundred yards away the trees grew thick and tall, like a fairy-tale forest. His legs were much longer than hers, and obviously stronger. She quickly grew short of breath from trying to keep up.

After a few minutes Daniel began to outpace her. She was too proud to ask him to wait, but somehow he seemed to sense that she was falling behind. He stopped, and, when she caught up, he reached back with his left hand.

"Hold on," he said. "This is steeper than it looks."

She grabbed his gloved hand gratefully, curling her fingers into his. "Aren't there any good trees growing *down* the mountain?" She hoped she didn't sound grumpy. After all, this whole expedition was for her benefit.

He glanced back at her with a smile. "Sure," he said. "But then we'd have to drag the tree home uphill."

"Oh. Right." She felt like a fool. Her breath was coming out in fast little puffs now, like a steam engine on overdrive, and her heart was pounding against the stupid spandex tunic that was so tight it flattened her breasts in a very unflattering manner. She supposed you had to be built like the delectable Doreen to look good in a ski outfit.

Or like Jocelyn, perhaps? It wasn't the first time she had wondered what Daniel's late wife had looked like. There wasn't a single picture on display in the lodge, but a portrait was taking shape in Lindsay's mind.

She must have been blond—the office gossips had told Lindsay that Alice was fair-haired. And dressed like a little princess—so obviously Jocelyn had been fashion-conscious, as well.

Well-dressed, tall and willowy, with long painted fingernails. Possessive of her man, but utterly confident. All in all, a rather intimidating character.

Of course, a defiant little voice inside her persisted, Jocelyn didn't sound all that *nice*...

But facts were facts. And it was a scientific fact that very darn few men would choose Miss Congeniality when they could have Miss American Man-Killer instead. *Give up*, she ordered herself. The touch in her bedroom had been her imagination. The kiss just now had been merely pity.

They were entering the forest, and, filtered through the trees, the light softened, crisscrossing in random beams through the branches.

Suddenly Daniel stopped. "Listen," he said, squeezing her hand.

She held her breath and frowned, wondering what he wanted her to hear. She couldn't detect a thing except the low, thrumming beat of her own heart. And then, after a minute, she understood. Listen, he had meant, to the silence.

Nothing broke the purity of it. No bird sang; no animal twittered. Nothing skittered in the treetops, rustling the leaves. Nothing dashed across the ground, crunching the snow underfoot. She and Daniel might have been the only two living creatures on earth.

"The blizzard has driven the animals to ground," he said, his voice hushed. He looked around curiously. "In a normal winter, this forest is teeming with life. Chipmunks, birds, squirrels, foxes. Lots of deer. Sometimes even a bear or two."

How magical it must be, she thought. "I wish I could see the deer," she whispered. "But it's okay with me if the bears keep right on sleeping."

He still held her hand, though there was no longer any need. She decided not to mention that, nestling her fingers deeper into the curve of his palm.

"We usually cut a fairly small tree, maybe five or six feet," he said, looking around. "We replant every year, so there should be a selection of all shapes and sizes."

"You always cut your own tree?" Envious, she thought of her own treks to the Phoenix tree lots, which usually were no more than canopies hung over the asphalt parking areas of abandoned filling stations. "Your daughter must have loved that."

She knew she was taking a chance to mention Alice, but it seemed unnatural, and unhealthy, too, that Daniel avoided the subject so completely. She understood his reluctance—she hadn't talked about her father for a long time after his death, either. But gradually she had accepted that you needed to air your memories every now and then in order to keep them fresh and clean.

Daniel's hand twitched slightly, but his voice was bland. "I suppose she did. Roc usually took her. I never could get away from the office in time."

"Never?"

"Never." Daniel stopped before a fir that was almost as tall as he was. "How about this one?" Letting go of her hand, he circled the tree. "No, I don't think so. The trunk isn't straight."

Lindsay surveyed the trees in the immediate vicinity. There were so many lovely ones that a decision seemed impossible. A few yards away, for instance, eight or ten beautiful trees seemed to have been planted in a circle. Taken together, their tall, irregular spires had the curious look of a Medieval castle.

"Look!" She pointed to the strange grouping. "Aren't they extraordinary?"

Daniel seemed to hesitate. "Yes," he said. "My sister and I used to play there. We thought it looked like an old abbey." He turned away, apparently disinterested. "Come on, now, let's see if we can't agree on *something* here."

Half an hour later, they were still looking, arguing spiritedly over every detail and enjoying every minute of what Daniel had decided was not a hunt but a quest. A quest for the perfect Christmas tree.

It wasn't the Holy Grail, but it might as well have been. This one was too tall, that one too short, another too scrawny, and many of them, according to Daniel, simply not shaped correctly.

"Nope," he said, shaking his head over the tree Lindsay was standing beside, her brows raised hopefully. "Too top heavy."

She rolled her eyes. "For a man who didn't even want to decorate at all, you're turning out to be mighty difficult to satisfy," she said. "If we're lucky, we might find one you approve of in time for Christmas *next* year."

"I'm not difficult," he said, grinning that insufferable grin and then walking away to check out another stand of trees. "I'm just particular."

"Yeah, I've noticed." She bent down and began to pack a softball-size snowball together. "You're *particularly* annoying." She lobbed the lumpy white missile toward his head.

She missed him by a mile, the snowball splatting against the trunk of a tree they'd rejected—she forgot why—half an hour earlier. He wheeled around, his eyes widening dangerously.

"Now *that*," he said slowly, "was not smart."

"Oh, yeah?" She bit her lower lip and tried to look tough. "Why not?"

He began to move toward her, his steps deliberate and sure across the deep snow. "Because you missed, that's why. The cardinal rule in a snowball fight is never fire until you see the white of their eyes. Haven't you ever heard that?"

"Hmm... It sounds familiar..." Lindsay backed up, intimidated in spite of herself by the sight of him stalking toward her. He looked like a lean, graceful black predator, covering the few yards of ground that lay between them with no effort at all. Irrationally, a bubble of fear tickled against her ribcage, and she kept backstepping until she felt the soft needles of a tree against her hair.

Cornered, she bent down to create another snowball, but she had just barely closed her hand around the snow before he was upon her. He took her by the shoulders and lifted her to a standing position.

He glanced at the snow in her hand. It was about the size of a golf ball, assuming there could ever be a lopsided, elliptical golf ball.

"Aw, Lindsay..." His voice was low, husky. "You weren't going to throw that at me, now were you?"

Smiling down into her eyes, he nudged her shoulders slowly until, off balance, she had to step back. Snow jostled free of the pine needles and fell like white rain on her arms. He pushed a little harder, moving her just a few more inches, until the soft branches parted under the weight of her body, and the pungent scent of pine exploded all around them.

He pressed again, until finally the firm rod of the tree's trunk met the curve of her spine. And then he stopped.

"Were you?" he asked again, running his hand down her arm, all the way to the hand that still gripped the deformed little snowball.

"I was thinking about it," she said, but the bravado of the words was undermined by the tremor in her voice.

"Don't," he said softly. "Not yet. There's something I want to tell you first." His gaze rested lightly on her lips, which made them tingle. "And then, if you still want to hit me, I promise I'll stand back and let you do it."

She could hardly keep her fist closed around the snow. Her whole arm felt too weak to grip. But she nodded as best she could. "All right," she agreed, bewildered, but too intoxicated by the smell of pine and the nearness of Daniel to try to sort it all out.

"I know it may seem sudden," he said, never taking his gaze from her face. "I just hope I can make you understand."

"What?" She licked her lips, which suddenly felt dry. "What is it?"

He reached up to brush a few flakes of snow from her hair. The rush of heat she felt should have been enough to melt any lingering snow right back to pure water.

"Have you ever been looking for something, something that is so important it seems you can't go on without it, and yet it always seems to elude you?"

She nodded, still bemused. "Yes, I suppose so."

"And sometimes you even think you may have found it, but, for one reason or another, it's not quite right? You know you have to keep on looking...until it's really perfect?" She nodded again, hypnotized by the sensual beauty of his deep voice. He smiled. "And then, just when you've almost given up hope, suddenly there it is, right in front of you."

She realized that she was holding her breath, hardly hearing his sentences, just watching his hard, full lips forming the words.

"That has just happened to me, Lindsay," he said.

"It has?" She still wasn't breathing.

"Yes," he said. "Right here. Right now."

He took her hand and, shaking the snow from her suddenly limp fingers, he slowly snaked it above her head, placing it palm down on the rigid column of the trunk. He slid her hand sensuously over the rough bark.

"I've found what I was looking for," he said, and, though it was far, far too late, she finally saw the mischief in his eyes. "I've found the perfect Christmas tree."

Two hours later, up in the attic hunting for Christmas ornaments, she still couldn't think back on that little trick without wanting to shove a handful of snow into his sweatpants. It had, in fact, initiated an all-out donnybrook, with snow flying wildly from both directions, lots of ridiculous running and stumbling and wrestling one another to the ground. The sound of their laughter had echoed in the crisp air like the peal of bells.

Afterward, they had sat, shoulder to shoulder for warmth, on a blanket he made of pine needles, and rested. The sky was clouding over, and the wind was growing stronger, but through the trees she could see the gray swirl of smoke rising from their chimney. The sight was like a promise...safety and comfort were waiting for them, whenever they were ready to come home.

Home. She was shocked to see how naturally the word sprang to mind. She wasn't sure when it had happened, but she suddenly realized she didn't feel like a prisoner on this mountain anymore. She felt as if she belonged here, with the snow and the trees and the freezing wind against her face. And Daniel at her side.

She slanted a glance at him. His cap had come off during the battle, and his dark hair had been tousled into a glamorous storm of loose waves around his face. Above his black turtleneck, his profile was clean and strong against the snow-gray sky. Though he wasn't smiling, he looked relaxed. He looked happy.

After that, the tree had been almost secondary, though it had indeed been perfectly beautiful, and it had yielded to his ax with almost no resistance. Together they had dragged it home in a companionable, tired silence.

Home, she thought again, with an internal shiver. How dangerous it was to let herself think such things. She stood up and prowled to another corner of the attic, where yet another unmarked cardboard box had been shoved up against the wall. This wasn't her home.

Apparently misinterpreting her quiet mood as they sat on the mountainside together, Daniel had turned to her, their eyes meeting solemnly. ''I'll get you home to Christy as soon as it's humanly possible,'' he had said unexpectedly, touching her knee with his black-gloved hand. And after all her carrying-on about getting back to Phoenix, what could she say? It could be tonight, if the ice storm didn't materialize...or tomorrow. At best, she had only three or four more days here. No, she had no right to think of this as home.

She sliced open the carton with a slow drag of the knife Daniel had given her. He had been right—Roc *had* saved it all. Underneath a sea of bright green tissue paper, boxes and boxes of ornaments lay waiting for someone to claim them. A shimmering pile of gold tree garlands had been stacked to one side. And on the other, strand upon strand of multicolored lights wound around each other.

And there, tucked in the back corner...what was that? Lindsay picked it up. It looked like a Christmas present, something flat and rectangular covered in giftwrap that showed kittens in Santa caps cavorting around a Christmas tree. Taped just beneath the big blue bow was a card. Four little words scrawled in a beginner's print. "To Daddy From Alice."

Lindsay inhaled sharply. Trying to make sense of it, she ran her hand slowly across the paper, touching each silly kitten separately. It obviously had never been opened. She couldn't believe Daniel even knew it was here. If he did, how could he have left it wrapped up all these years? Surely he would have wanted to see any gift from his lost daughter, to hold it and cherish it as the last thing she would ever give him.

No, it must be that Roc had put it up here himself, without even telling Daniel of its existence. But why? She pressed her fingers against the edges, wondering what it could be. Why? Had Roc known what it was, known that, for some reason, no comfort for Daniel lay inside?

Slowly, with a feeling of hollow sadness, she slipped the package behind one of the other boxes along the wall. If Roc had decided that Daniel mustn't see the gift, then Lindsay couldn't overrule him. It wasn't any of her business, no matter how much she might wish it could be.

Luckily, the box of decorations wasn't heavy. She was able to pick it up herself and carefully back down the narrow stairs from the attic. At the second-story landing she set the box down and leaned over the banister. "I found it," she called.

Daniel appeared at the foot of the steps immediately. "Good timing," he said. "I've just managed to get the tree secured. Apparently I was wrong. It's not perfect. Its trunk makes a damned inconvenient right turn about two-thirds of the way up."

But he didn't look particularly upset. His expression was still carefree, the way it had been on the mountain, and Lindsay felt her own mood begin to rise again in response. She had been right, hadn't she? Decorating the house was just a small step, but it would help Daniel find his way out of the darkness.

In the great room, Lindsay stopped, stunned by the size and beauty of the tree they had brought home. Out on the mountainside, surrounded by so many huge, ancient trees, this one had seemed rather small, almost insignificant.

Now she saw how astute Daniel's choice had been. The tree was about six and a half feet high, scaling gracefully to the corner he'd chosen. It was elegant rather than cute, attenuated rather than chubby—a tall, flawless pyramid that tapered with exquisite perfection to its starry peak.

"Like it?" He dug through the box, setting aside the ornaments and garlands. When he came to the strings of colored lights, he hauled out a couple of bulky knots and began searching for an end to pull.

"Of course," she said softly, moving in to touch the soft, firred branches. She remembered how those branches had tickled against her hair. "It's magnificent."

"Okay, then, how about helping with this?" She looked up just in time to see him tossing the tangled ball of cord toward her.

She caught it up against her chest, wondering where on earth to begin unraveling. "It seems sort of futile to put these on, doesn't it?" She touched the cold glass of a blue bulb, thinking what a lovely light it would have made. "After all, we don't have any electricity, remember?"

"What a practical lady you are!" Daniel glanced up from his labors, a small smile quirking one corner of his mouth. "Who's to say the power won't be back on by Christmas?"

He plugged his strand into the dead electrical socket and began threading it into the tree. When she didn't join him, he looked over at her again.

"What's the matter, Lindsay? Don't you believe in miracles?"

CHAPTER NINE

THE ice storm hit at midnight. An angry wind howled past the lodge for hours, and bullets of icy rain pelted the windows. Daniel and Lindsay sat in the candlelit great room together, neither one suggesting that they retire. The rest of the house, including its three bedrooms, might not have existed.

In spite of the fury outside, Lindsay felt safe, as if the lodge were under a magic spell that rendered it invulnerable. The walls groaned beneath the wind's onslaught, and occasionally something would clatter across the roof, but she felt no fear. Now and then a finger of wet wind found its way down the chimney, and the fire crackled angrily at the intrusion, spitting sprays of glowing red embers into the room. But Lindsay merely thought it was beautiful.

Their tree, too, was gorgeous by firelight. The thick golden garlands that looped over the branches seemed almost alive. Each shivering metallic strand threw back a hundred shimmering reflections. Enchanted, she hardly noticed that the electric lights remained cold and colorless.

As though by unspoken consent, they had decided not to play chess. Instead they read magazines; Daniel did a little paperwork; they snacked from a plate of cold cuts and vegetables Lindsay had set out on the coffee table; and then for hours they talked desultorily of trivial, fascinating things.

Finally, though she would have liked the evening to go on forever, Lindsay's eyes grew heavy. She put her feet up on the sofa, rested her head against the padded arm, and fell asleep in the middle of a conversation about Indian legends.

She felt as if only a moment passed. Suddenly Daniel was kneeling beside her, touching her arm.

"Wake up, sleepyhead," he said softly.

The silence was the first thing she noticed. The storm, she realized, was over. She lifted herself up on one elbow. "What is it?" she said groggily.

She looked over her shoulder to see whether it was day or night. It seemed to be something in between. The sky was a slate gray, marbled with dusky rose and tangerine tints. She yawned and stretched and closed her eyes again. What was Daniel thinking? It wasn't quite dawn yet.

"Hey, you—it's time to get up," he said, massaging her hand. "I want to show you something."

"Ummmm." She smiled, but she didn't open her eyes. "What?"

"Up." With very little help from her, Daniel eased her to a sitting position and slipped her arms into Doreen's yellow ski jacket.

"Oh, no," she said, finally waking up enough to realize what he was doing. "We're not going outside, are we?" He nodded, and she sighed heavily, rubbing her eyes. "This better be worth it," she warned him.

It was.

The entire world had been transformed in the night. The trees were no longer thick and lumpy with snow. Now they gleamed like exquisite crystal sculptures, too detailed to be real, too poignantly fragile to last. Each tiny leaf and pine needle, each intricate design of bare twig, had been individually covered in clear, glistening ice. The whole landscape seemed to be made of the purest glass that caught the colored lights from the dawn.

A thick coating of crystalline rime covered the ground, too. It was easier to walk now, as long as she didn't slip. She clung to Daniel, and in a few short minutes they were back in the forest, looking at the circle of trees she had pointed out to him yesterday.

"We called it the Crystal Abbey," he said, taking her hand in his and leading her, speechless, toward the strange, beautiful form created by the storm.

She supposed it was technically white, and yet somehow it appeared to be made of multicolored prisms. She could see immediately why he called it an abbey. The intricate webs of icy branches grew so close together that they seemed to interlock, making walls. The spires of the larger trees rose like fantasy steeples from either end, gleaming a clear, crystal pink in the dawn.

"Look from this side." Putting his hand on her back, he shifted her a couple of feet to the left. "See those two tallest trees on the right? Some of their branches broke off years ago, and now there's an arched gap between them. See it?"

She nodded, finding the space easily. She could glimpse the dawn sky through the opening, its mottled colors like swirls of oil paint on a palette.

"That's the stained-glass window over the north transept," he said, a touch of laughter in his voice. "Or so we thought when we were about ten. My sister and I used to play here when we were little. We liked to pretend it was a haunted monastery. My sister was the abbess." He put his hand on her back, urging her to walk around the perimeter. "I had to play the mad monk."

They made the full circle. From every angle, the abbey was equally lovely. "Does this happen every winter?" she asked, awed.

"No. I've seen it like this six or eight times, I suppose." He touched one of the glittering branches. "It only happens after a major ice storm. The last one was about five years ago.''

Five years ago. His daughter would have been alive then. Lindsay counted back—Alice would have been about four, the perfect age. Perhaps that accounted for the strangely poignant note in Daniel's voice, she thought. Perhaps he had last been here with Alice.

''I'll bet your daughter loved it,'' she said tentatively, still hoping to draw something out of him. It might smack of pop psychology, but she instinctively knew it would do him good to talk about it.

His face tightened. ''She never saw it,'' he said in a monotone, still fingering the icy twig, studying it. ''We didn't come to the lodge that Christmas. I was closing a deal in San Francisco.''

Lindsay's heart sank deep into her chest. Another stupid blunder. Wouldn't she ever learn to mind her own business? ''I'm sorry,'' she said.

He snapped the twig from its branch like an icicle. He rolled the broken piece through his fingers for a long moment before he spoke. Lindsay watched. It looked like a fossil, this sad piece of wood encased in its glass coffin.

''Lindsay, listen,'' he said finally, his voice gruff. ''If you're trying to get me to start pouring out sentimental reminiscences about the idyllic days I spent with Alice, you might as well give up. I don't have any memories like that.''

She looked over at him, stricken. How bitter he sounded! Not any? Had he never spent any time with the little girl at all?

''To put it simply, I was a rotten father,'' he said, walking a few feet away from her, his feet crunching on the crust of ice.

She wanted to cry out an instinctive denial. He couldn't have been. She had seen him with Roc, and she had felt his tenderness herself just yesterday, when she had been in tears over Christy. This wasn't a heartless man. This wasn't a man who didn't know how to love. Surely with his own daughter...

But something in his posture stopped her. He stood with a hopeless rigidity, like an unarmed man facing down an old enemy. He looked into the middle distance as if he searched for something there, and he took a deep breath.

"My marriage was a mess, almost from the beginning. Jocelyn and I couldn't be in the same house for five minutes without arguing, so I practically lived at the office. She didn't give a damn about me, but her ego couldn't take rejection. She retaliated by shutting me out of Alice's life as much as she could."

He glanced at Lindsay, his eyes hooded. "I don't offer that as an excuse. I didn't fight very hard, I'm afraid. By then I was sick of the fighting. And somehow, gradually, I guess we just all got used to living apart."

Lindsay tucked her hands into her pockets, for the first time aware of the intense cold. No wonder he never spoke of this. It must be almost unendurable.

"Anyhow, Jocelyn loved to tell me how much Alice resented me—even hated me—for being gone so much. And I'm quite certain that was true. Jocelyn would have made sure of it."

"Oh, no, Alice couldn't have hated you," Lindsay protested in spite of her determination to remain silent. She couldn't bear that desolate quality in his voice. "Jocelyn probably said that just to hurt you. Believe me, it's pretty hard to make a little girl hate her daddy."

Deep in the jacket pockets, her hands balled in fists. She was beginning to despise the faceless, elegant Jocelyn, who had dared to poison a little girl's mind against her father.

"You underestimate our Jocelyn," he said dully. "She was a master of alienation. And remember, she was getting plenty of help from me. I never went along for the shopping trips, the ballet recitals, the parties. I just wasn't there."

"You brought her to the office," Lindsay said. "Everyone heard about that."

He smiled, but it was as cold as the frozen prisms of the abbey walls.

"Yes. And what a joke that was! I thought she needed some experiences that didn't involve the mall or the beauty salon. Jocelyn was hell-bent on making Alice into a miniature of herself." Suddenly his brow furrowed, and his jaw clenched. "She did look just like her mother. She was going to be a beauty."

He passed his hand over his forehead, as if to clear the images away. "I guess the real truth was that the office was the one place where I could spend time with Alice without having to include Jocelyn. My wife would rather have been dragged over hot coals than think about business. But it was a selfish decision. A corporate board meeting is hardly a six-year-old's idea of fun."

"You don't know that," Lindsay said. Impulsively, she walked over to him, as if by closing the physical space between them she could close the emotional distance, as well. "She was your daughter, too, with your genes. Maybe, with enough time, she would have learned to love the business. She might even have joined you in it someday."

He looked at her a long time, unreadable expressions shifting across his face.

"That's a nice thought," he said finally. He reached up and touched her cheek, briefly, with one gloved finger. "But somehow it doesn't surprise me, coming from you. You're a very nice person, Lindsay Blaisdell."

She flushed, her cold cheeks suddenly flaming. "Don't dismiss me like that," she said. "I'm not just being polite. I meant what I said."

One corner of his mouth rose slightly. "Is that what you think I'm doing? Dismissing you?"

"Yes," she said, frustrated, but somehow unable to articulate exactly why. When he had said it was a "nice thought," it had sounded patronizing, the way he might have said that world peace was a nice thought, or a cure for cancer.

But that wasn't really what bothered her. If she were being honest, she'd have to admit that most of all she hated to hear how "nice" he thought she was. Nice was such a tame, boring word...

"Well, are you?" She looked up at him, and her gaze locked with his. "Are you dismissing me, Daniel?"

He smiled.

"I'm trying to," he said, shaking his head slowly. "God knows I'm trying."

It was hardly the answer she'd been hoping for, but suddenly her heart felt as light as the rainbows that flashed from the abbey's walls. She turned away, unwilling to let him see the emotion that overwhelmed her.

"Well, aren't you ever going to invite me in?" She touched the nearly solid wall of ice. "I don't see any doors. Have they grown over through the years?"

"Ah...for that you have to know the secret," Daniel said, his voice mysterious. He walked a few feet to his left. Suddenly he seemed to disappear, slipping as if by magic through the ice.

Mystified, she followed. And then she saw what he had done. At one edge of the circle, the trees didn't line up exactly right. From a distance, the branches appeared to close tightly, but actually they left an opening through which a person could pass.

"Coming?" Only Daniel's head was still visible, and the gloved hand he held out toward her, palm up, beckoning.

"Of course."

"Are you sure you dare? Remember—it's haunted."

She let her fingers close over his. "I've never been afraid of ghosts."

Even so, she shut her eyes as he drew her through the narrow passage. Her hair caught on some of the icy tentacles, and tiny tinkling sounds rang out as icicles broke off and hit the ground.

Once inside, she opened her eyes slowly, and exhaled a soft, disbelieving sigh. The dawn light poured in from all sides, suffusing the entire area in a rosy glow. Above them the sky streamed with long, rippled pennants of pink and blue. She felt as if she had stepped inside a dream. Daniel's dream.

"It's the most beautiful place I've ever seen," she said breathlessly, twirling to take in every amazing inch of it. "And the most peaceful."

She looked up at him. "I don't think there are any ghosts here, Daniel."

The light bathed everything, even Daniel himself. He stared at her with a solemn gaze, and she wondered whether she, too, glowed with that same rosy hue.

"You may be right," he said slowly. "You may have chased them away, at least for today."

"Why just for today?" She moved closer to him, so close their jackets touched. She could hardly breathe. "Perhaps they won't ever come back."

His eyes darkened. With a muffled groan he reached for her.

"Today is enough," he said roughly, though his hands were gentle in her hair, on her shoulders, down her back. "Today is more than I ever expected to have."

He kissed her then, and his kiss tasted strangely pink, like the dawn, like cherries and roses and sweet melted rubies. Murmuring her name against her lips, he closed his arms around her tightly, and she held him, too, thrilling in the warmth of him, the strength of him, her overwhelming need of him.

They sank to their knees, and from there he laid her against the floor of ice, pillowing her head with his arm. He combed his gloved fingers into her hair and allowed his kiss to deepen, his hard lips nudging hers apart, demanding that she let him enter, breathing his honeyed fire into her very soul.

Moaning, she swept her hands across his shoulders, down his chest, trying to find the connection she craved. She longed to feel the firm swell of his muscles beneath her fingers, the pulsing heat of his blood beneath her palms. But her gloves and his jacket formed an impenetrable barrier. The fabrics that had been designed to keep out the cold were too clever, too strong, and she whimpered, needing more, needing to know if his body burned beneath this armor, just as hers did.

He silenced the small, desperate sound with his mouth, going deeper still, his tongue hot and sweet against her teeth, against the sensitive inner rim of her lips, and finally, thrillingly, against the tip of her own tongue. Colors flashed through her veins, as if she had become a prism herself.

It was the most glorious kiss she had ever known, stirring erotic desires she had never felt before. But it wasn't enough. All the thwarted need in both their bodies had been concentrated in this one bruising kiss, this inadequate inch where flesh was allowed to press against flesh.

He pulled back slowly, as if he dreaded the moment when their lips finally parted. His breath came fast, misting in the air like a flag of passion. His eyes were so dark, the blue was almost smothered. She licked her lips, which were suddenly numb, needing him to warm them again.

With his free hand he slipped the snaps of her jacket loose and folded the edges back. Then, with one graceful motion, he slid the zipper of her tunic open, from throat to navel. He pulled the fabric of her undershirt away from her breasts, and she gasped as the air rushed into caress her with icy fingers.

"Daniel," she cried, frightened by the intensity of the sensation. She was cold, so cold it was almost unbearable, and she clutched at his arms, breathing shallowly. As he shifted, a small current of frigid air swirled over her. Her skin tightened, as if he had touched her.

Slowly, he bent his head and let his warm lips graze the pebbled tip of her breast. She twisted in his arms, seeking the comfort those lips promised. His soft breath streamed in a heated mist over her skin, and the moist touch of his tongue was like a burn against her icy skin.

And then, hungrily, he pulled her into the hot darkness of his mouth. An electrical current jolted through her, aching her back and tightening every muscle to the breaking point. She buried her hands in his hair and somehow managed not to cry out.

But as his mouth grew more demanding, a shiver began to build inside her, like the slight tremors of the earth before it splits and quakes. Strange that she should begin to tremble now, she thought from a great distance. It wasn't a reaction to the cold, although she was cold, terribly, everywhere except where he touched her. No, this shivering had begun from the inside, from somewhere in the silent, unseen heart of her. It was more like a fever of the blood, involuntary and unstoppable.

Suddenly, explosively, the tremors pulsed their way to the surface. A fine haze of gooseflesh prickled along her skin, and the muscles in her upper arms began to tremble. She clenched her stomach, trying to still the motions before Daniel could sense them.

But he was too aware, too sensitive to her responses. Before she could bring the tiny shivers under control, he had already pulled away, looking down at her with dark and cloudy eyes. With the heat of him withdrawn, her shaking intensified.

"Lindsay," he breathed, folding her quickly up against him, rubbing his hands across her back roughly. "Oh, God, Lindsay, I'm sorry."

"No," she whispered, though she could hardly speak. Her jaw felt paralyzed from the effort to keep her shoulders from shaking. "No, I'm all right."

"Like hell you are. You're half frozen," he said, and his voice held an undercurrent of anger. Somehow, though, she knew he was angry with himself, not with her. "What a damned fool I am..."

Cursing under his breath, he stood, pulling her to her feet along with him. With hurried motions that were still amazingly deft, he tugged her undershirt down and pushed it under the waistband of her trousers. Then, with one lightning stroke, he thrust her tunic's zipper up the length of her torso, closing it tightly around her neck.

"We'd better get you inside," he said, his tone painfully impersonal. He found her cap, which had tumbled onto the ice, and he placed it gently over her head, tucking her hair up into it. His eyes were dark as he searched her face. "You're as pale as ice."

Gradually, her body seemed to be coming back under her own control. Finally, when she believed that she could speak coherently, she put her hand on his arm, praying that she could make him understand.

"I wasn't cold," she said and then hesitated, unsure exactly how to express without sounding hopelessly gauche the eruptions of desire that had overtaken her. After all, it wasn't as if they had made mad, passionate love here on the ice. An unzipped zipper—that was as far as it had gone... Hardly enough to make the earth move. And yet, somehow, the terrain of her soul had shifted. It would never, she sensed, be the same again.

He raised his brows, tracing the goose bumps along her collarbone with his forefinger. "You weren't?"

She shook her head. "No. I just—" She swallowed, and she could feel his finger at the base of her throat, where it had paused in its path. "I just wanted you."

His lips tightened. "And I wanted you," he said, but there was no indication that either her admission or his pleased him at all.

Sighing, he dropped his hand to his side. "In fact, I wanted you so much that I was ready to forget everything else."

"Like what?" She heard the need that still vibrated under her words. "What else mattered?"

"How about the fact that it's five degrees below zero?" He smiled a rueful half smile, and reaching out again slowly, as if against his will, he touched her cheek. "Or the fact that wanting you doesn't give me the right to take you whenever and however I choose."

As she began to protest, he slid his finger over her lips, silencing her. "And I was ready to forget the most important thing of all," he said in a voice so sad it made her ache inside. "Today's fantasies, however lovely, don't last forever, Lindsay. Tomorrow's ugly realities always show up to destroy them sooner or later.''

Daniel monitored the radio's weather channel all afternoon, placing frequent calls to the airport to check on flying conditions. After the scene in the abbey, he knew he needed to get Lindsay out of here before he did something really stupid. She was so sweet, so willing, so desirable. And he, apparently, was so weak. He felt like Adam, fatally fixated on the one forbidden fruit in the whole godforsaken garden.

But the weather wouldn't cooperate. It was almost dark, and he had just heard that small plane warnings remained in effect until 3:00 a.m. tomorrow, Christmas morning. The Littledale bridge would remain down through New Year's Day. Therefore, Lindsay Blaisdell remained in his house, ironically under his protection and disastrously under his skin, for at least one more long, tempting night.

Even worse, she didn't seem to appreciate how heroic his self-control had been this morning. Her eyes were cloudy when she looked at him, which didn't happen as often as it had yesterday. That was a real loss...he missed her open, sunny smiles more than he could have imagined.

And her voice was flat when she talked to him, an event that had also become increasingly infrequent as the stilted afternoon progressed. Another loss... he had enjoyed her company. Just these few days of it had spoiled him for the solitude he used to crave.

He had hurt her, there was no question about it. She was rotten at hiding her feelings, and her embarrassed pain was as plainly visible as the straight little nose on her face. Or the full, sensual lips. Or the wide, blue eyes.

All of which he'd like to kiss quite thoroughly. Right here. Right now.

Damnation. He flung his pen down on the desk, and it clanked loudly against the paperweight. She looked up from her magazine, a quizzical frown between her eyes, but she didn't ask what was the matter. Obviously she thought she knew. She thought he wanted to be rid of her.

Which he did.

Didn't he?

He growled under his breath and stood up, staring out the window at the trees, which were still visible by the dying sunset. They swayed dramatically in the high winds, as if to remind him that the weather had no plans to improve.

When the telephone rang, he snatched it up with a sense of relief all out of proportion to the event.

It was Roc.

"Looks like you sent me packing for nothing, Danny Boy," the older man said, as usual ignoring the customary opening courtesies. "That mangy collection of pill-pushers and bone-benders you sent me to couldn't find a darn thing wrong with me, so they had to just sew me up and send me home."

Daniel had already known that, of course, but he didn't let on that he'd been keeping in constant contact with the hospital. "They couldn't find anything wrong with you? May I assume, then, that they didn't let the psychiatrists look?"

Lindsay glanced up, apparently realizing who was on the line. For the first time in hours, her face was bright with pleasure. Daniel squelched a twinge of annoyance. Why should she mope all afternoon with him, then light up like a Christmas tree for Roc, who was perhaps the most annoying, irascible man on earth?

"Head-peepers?" Roc made a rude noise. "What good would that do? Those quacks couldn't find their—"

"Rump with a compass," Daniel finished for him. "I know, I know."

"Yeah, well, excuse me if my routine is boring you. I didn't call to talk to your sorry self anyway. Is Miss Lindsay still there, or have you let her get away like the fool that you are?"

Daniel flicked a glance toward the sofa, where Lindsay sat, still smiling, apparently hanging on his every word, hoping for details about Roc's condition. "She's here," he said cautiously. "We've had bad luck with the weather."

"Bad luck?" Roc sounded incredulous. "*Bad* luck? I swear, I'm starting to think you're a hopeless case, Danny Boy. A comatose priest would have caught on to what a classy dame that girl is faster than you have."

"You're wrong, Roc." Daniel paused. "I'm well aware of that."

"Well, thank God for something!" Roc chuckled, obviously self-satisfied. "So. What're you going to do about it?"

"Nothing."

"*Nothing?*" Roc's indignant bellow reverberated against Daniel's eardrum. "*Nothing?*"

"That's right."

Roc sputtered another moment, and then he sighed tragically. "Fine. Be a chowderhead if that's what makes you happy. I give up. Put Miss Lindsay on the phone."

Daniel almost refused. There was no telling what Roc might decide to say. He certainly seemed to be in high form tonight. But in the end he could no more deny Roc the pleasure of talking to Lindsay than he could resist that hopeful smile on Lindsay's face.

He held out the telephone. "It's Roc," he said. "He wants to talk to you."

She took it eagerly, asking all the right, affectionate questions, laughing at all Roc's undoubtedly lame witticisms. But after a few moments her comments turned guarded, just as Daniel's had been. He stared at the papers on his desk, pretending not to listen. Wishing he didn't want to listen. She was very discreet. He couldn't even begin to piece together a conversation from the monosyllabic responses he heard at her end.

After what seemed like ages, she told Roc a warm goodbye and then handed the telephone back to Daniel. "I'm just going to go upstairs," she said politely. "I'll be back down in a few minutes."

He worked on the fire while she was gone, adding and rearranging logs, trying not to speculate too much on what Roc might have told her. And trying, too, not to miss her, not to notice how bleak the room seemed now that she wasn't in it.

Finally he heard her coming down the stairs. Turning, he saw that she was inching toward him slowly, almost as if she were afraid to approach him. Up against her chest she held what appeared to be a Christmas present. He felt a sting of shame. Where had she acquired that? He hadn't given a single thought to putting together a present for her...

When she was close enough to be within the range of the firelight, he could see that the thing she held was indeed wrapped in Christmas paper. He squinted. Christmas kittens, if he saw correctly. It looked like a child's wrapping paper.

"This has been in the attic for the past three years," she said. Her voice was uncertain, a low tremor below the words. "Roc thinks I should give it to you now."

Something cold closed around his heart like a fist. She was holding out the present, face up so that he could see the big blue bow. And he could see the card that had been taped beneath it.

"To Daddy," the card said. The fist squeezed him harder, so hard he had to fight the urge to double over. "To Daddy From Alice."

CHAPTER TEN

LINDSAY said a silent prayer that Roc had made the right decision. His logic had seemed odd, to say the least. He had left the unopened gift in the attic with the Christmas decorations, he said, because he knew that when Daniel was emotionally ready to have a real Christmas, then he would be ready to see the present, too.

But that equation sounded more superstitious than scientific. What if he was wrong? Had he factored in Lindsay's presence? After all, Daniel hadn't decided to trim a Christmas tree this year just because he felt a sudden burst of Yuletide cheer. He had done it to ease Lindsay's homesickness. Couldn't that fatally skew Roc's calculations?

Looking at Daniel's hard face now, Lindsay felt a squirm of anxiety. The sun had gone down, and his features were gray in the rising moonlight. He made no move to reach for the package, standing instead with his hands apparently frozen at his sides.

"Daniel, please." She stepped closer, holding the gift out so far it almost touched the soft cashmere of his blue sweater. "Won't you open it?"

Though it clearly required an effort of will, he finally put out one hand stiffly and took it. He turned it over, then over again, studying both sides of the inexpertly wrapped rectangle as if he'd never seen a gift before. He ran his fingers over the shiny loops of the bow, pressing them flat, then watching them spring back into their original shape.

But he didn't open it.

She wiped her moist palms on her skirt. "Do you want me to leave you alone for a while?" She gestured toward the kitchen. "I could go get us something to eat."

"No." He looked up, his eyes glittering in the moonlight. "Stay."

He moved toward the firelight, where the illumination was better, and sat on the edge of the sofa, still looking down at the box.

"Roc's making a production over nothing here. Jocelyn picked out every present Alice ever gave me." Bitterness tightened his voice. "And believe me she didn't waste much of her precious time—or her money—doing it. It's probably just a box of cheap handkerchiefs."

Somehow Lindsay knew it was just his fear talking. He didn't dare to hope that this gift held anything personal, anything that might bring his lost Alice back to him, even for a moment. If he let himself hope, the disappointment might be too cruel.

She sat down on the sofa, fighting the urge to touch him, to reassure him. In her heart of hearts, she believed he was wrong. She had held the box, and it didn't feel as though Jocelyn's cold, impersonal imprint were on it.

At that, she gave herself a mental shake. Good grief, that was even more superstitious than Roc's reasoning! She tried to be rational, specific. The wrapping was clumsy, as if it had been folded by a child. The bow, which didn't quite match the paper, was affixed decidedly off center. Such trivial details, so little to pin such big hopes on...

Abruptly, as if disgusted by his own indecision, Daniel ripped into the wrapping paper, tearing it from top to bottom in one violent motion. Lindsay held her breath as he pulled the paper away and let it fall unnoticed on the carpet.

The present looked like a picture of some kind. She couldn't see it clearly—from her angle the glass in the frame caught a glare from the firelight, obscuring the details. Her mind raced—a picture? Of whom? Alice? Daniel? Jocelyn? All three of them together? She wondered whether she would be able to bear looking at that . . .

Daniel was utterly immobile. Not the smallest muscular twitch betrayed his reaction to what he had uncovered. He seemed to study it a long minute, and then, without speaking, he handed it to Lindsay and stood up, as if he could no longer relax enough to remain seated.

"Oh," she said, stunned into incoherence by what she saw. "Oh, Daniel . . ."

It wasn't a photograph at all. It was a crayon drawing, approximately eight-by-ten, done on the kind of paper children used at school for art projects. "Alice McKinley," it said in the top right corner, in the standard elementary school heading. "First Grade, Mrs. Beeman."

For a six-year-old's work, the picture was quite good. Lindsay recognized the setting immediately. It had to be the large conference room adjacent to Daniel's office. Several rather small, anonymous stick figures sat around the huge oak boardroom table, but the drawing was thoroughly dominated by the two people who sat at the head of that table, sharing the power position.

Loving attention had been given to every detail of these two figures. A tall man with ebony hair and aquamarine eyes, dressed in a black suit and a blue tie. A little girl whose long, straight blond hair was pulled back with an Alice in Wonderland blue headband, wearing a navy blue dotted swiss dress, beneath which a yellow crinoline peeked. Father and daughter, smiling at one another as if the rest of the people in the room had ceased to exist.

The picture had no words, no title, no arrows that pointed to the figures and named them. But it spoke volumes nonetheless. Lindsay touched the little girl's beaming smile, and her own eyes filled unexpectedly with grateful tears.

Whatever fears Daniel had harbored must surely be dispelled by this eloquent drawing. Alice McKinley had, without question, loved, and felt loved by, her father. These mutually proud, possessive smiles were proof of that.

She looked up, hoping to see her own relief reflected on Daniel's face. But he had turned away from her, one arm propped on the mantel, staring into the fire.

"What a wonderful gift," she said, wiping away her tears before he could see them. It might seem that she was taking his tragedy too personally. He would never understand how important his happiness was to her. "That day must have been very special to Alice."

"I suppose so," he said slowly. "I'm very glad of that."

But he didn't sound glad. He sounded numb. With a muffled groan, she stood and went to him, driven by frustration, by the fear that this blackness would never lift from his heart.

"What *is* it, Daniel?" She put both her hands on his arm, trying to make him look at her. "I know the loss of your daughter is terrible...worse than anything I could ever imagine. But it's been *three years*. Why can't you take even a tiny bit of happiness in this—" she shook the frame in her fist "—this miraculous gift that has been handed to you? Why do you continue to torment yourself?"

He still didn't look up. He simply shook his head with slow, deliberate movements. "Because it was my fault," he said dully. "It was my fault she died."

His fault? Surely he couldn't mean that literally. She searched her mind for any details she had read about the deaths. Blinded by the blizzard, Jocelyn had run off the road, into an embankment. The heavy snowfall had quickly covered the automobile, and all the traces of their route. By the time anyone realized they had gone, it had been almost impossible for rescuers to find them. Heartbreaking, tragic... but surely no one's *fault*.

"Why?" The hoarse syllable was all she could manage.

"Because you were right," he said, finally lifting his head to look at her. She was shocked to see the haunted pain in his glistening eyes. "Remember what you said the day I fired you? You said that Jocelyn was probably running away from me. Well, you were right."

She was bewildered. She hadn't known Daniel, or Jocelyn, or anything about them, not really. She had merely been venting her own desperate anger. She had simply been afraid that her grandmother would take Christy away, and she had said the first cruel thing that came to mind.

"What do you mean?" She took her hands away from his arm. "I've explained that to you, haven't I? I was terribly upset. I hardly knew what I was saying."

"Still, you were absolutely right," he said. "Jocelyn was leaving me. It was almost Christmas, remember? She and Alice had been staying here at the lodge."

He laughed, a black, bitter sound. "I was stuck in Phoenix—on business, of course... wasn't I always? Anyway, Roc had just called me, to warn me about... some things that Alice had told him. Things about Jocelyn's other men... lots of them..." He made a low, animal sound. "One of the sleazy bastards had dared to hit Alice when she came out of her room at an inopportune moment."

Lindsay gasped.

"Roc knew I didn't give a damn how many men Jocelyn slept with," he said, a dangerous edge sharpening his voice. "But he also knew I wouldn't let anyone on this earth lay a hand on my daughter. In a blind rage I called Jocelyn, and I told her that I was going to divorce her. I told her I was going to take Alice away from her."

Dread seeped into Lindsay like a slow, cold syrup. Her heart dragged at her chest. She didn't speak because she couldn't. Her vocal cords seemed to have lost their power.

"What a fool I was to warn her!" He rubbed his hands roughly across his face. When he removed them, his eyes no longer shone in the firelight, but they were even more frightening. They looked dry. Dead. "I knew how defiant she was. I should have realized that she wouldn't sit around waiting after a threat like that. But I stupidly assumed she had no choice. A blizzard was blowing in. Sure that she was imprisoned by the weather, I decided to attend one last meeting. One more useless, goddamn meeting!"

He looked at her from those blank, terrible eyes. "Can you believe the blind arrogance of it? God help me, I even remember thinking it might do Jocelyn good to have to stew for a while. To have to sit up here and regret the things she had done to Alice."

Lindsay shuddered, her eyes filling with hot tears. "But she didn't..."

"No. Of course she didn't." Daniel drew in a ragged breath. "She packed a bag, and then she put Alice in the car and roared away. She left a furious, hateful note telling me she was never coming back. She said that she would tell everyone, including any judge I cared to bring into this, what a terrible husband and father I was. That, if I dared to try to take our daughter away, I would never see Alice again."

His voice shook from the violence of the memory. A pulse throbbed in his jaw. "Two days later the mountain rescue team found them. Both of them were dead."

Oh, God... Lindsay tried to speak, but her throat was too thick to allow words to pass. She felt a burning trail of tears slipping down her cheeks. Oh, Daniel...

Blindly she reached out for him, seeking to comfort him in the only way she knew how—by offering herself to him, by laying down her soul as a place for him to rest his broken heart. She pressed herself against him, seeking not an embrace but a physical melding, an absolute union that would allow her to take the agony from his body into hers.

For one shattering moment he accepted her, opening himself to her so completely that she could almost feel the fusion taking place. His pain was her pain, and she welcomed it.

"Lindsay—" With a low moan, he buried his face in her hair, whispering things she couldn't hear, half words that were spoken in some hybrid language, a blend of desperation and desire.

But she didn't need to hear the words. She could feel the longing in his hands as clearly as she could feel the sorrow in his heart. She knew the rending need that ran through him like a fissure through parched earth. He needed her. He wanted her. Only in her could he find the peace he had lived so long without. She opened further, letting her body tell him that he could take whatever he needed.

But then, with a shudder, he pulled back. Lindsay sobbed once, a low, piercing sound, as if something had been physically torn from her body.

"No," he said, raking his hands through his hair. "I can't let you do this."

"Why not?" she asked, pressing her hands against his chest, trying to find the rhythm of his heart. She needed that low throb—it seemed to fuel her own heartbeat. Without it she was lost. "You want me. I can feel it."

"Of course I want you," he said roughly. "How could I help it? You're as warm as the sun, and I'm like some frozen, mindless creature programmed to turn toward the heat of you."

"Is that so wrong?" she asked. She took his hand. "I love you, Daniel," she said, not caring how it sounded, how vulnerable it made her. "I want to be the warmth you turn to."

For a moment he didn't speak. But then, with a low, helpless moan, he dragged her back into his arms. He slid his hands down her back and pressed her hips into him. She could feel him, hard and ready beneath the fleecy covering of his pants.

"We will warm each other," he vowed thickly. He cupped his hands against the edges of her hips, shifting her to fit against him. "Can you feel the fire, Lindsay? It burns in both of us tonight."

A thrill of expectation shot through her like a flaming arrow. Nodding breathlessly, she lifted her face to his. His kiss tasted of salt and heat and hunger. She murmured against the burning touch, an answering hunger rising in her, like a gnawing emptiness that demanded to be filled.

He pulled her sweater over her head, her dark hair tumbling around her bare shoulders. Then he slipped the clasp of her skirt, and it sank to the floor like melted wax from a burning candle. With the firelight flickering against her nakedness, he picked her up and gently laid her against the cushions of the sofa.

She watched as he undressed, hypnotized by the emerging masculine power. Desire curled inside her, like the coiling ash of a fast-burning wick. Her muscles seemed to be caught in a spiral of need that was tightening in on itself with every breath she took.

What was happening to her? She had never felt anything remotely like this wild yearning before. Even as she asked the question, though, she knew the answer. As crazy as it sounded, as impossible as it seemed, she loved this beautiful, tragic man—more than she had ever thought it was possible to love anyone. In less than a week, his happiness had come to mean more to her than her own.

But, amazingly, the act of love she was about to offer him would not require that she choose between his happiness and hers. She wanted him as fiercely as he wanted her.

With just a few tantalizing bends and stretches of his lean, graceful body, he shed his clothing. Sighing, she held out her arms to pull him close. She ran her hands along the velvet fire of his skin, and he mirrored her caresses with his own roaming, probing fingers. She moaned as he touched the tingling peaks of her breasts, cried out as he descended to the aching shadows between her legs.

Something powerful simmered in the deepest core of her, and instinct told her there would be no release until he ignited that waiting spark. She pressed herself against the length of him, but it still wasn't enough. She needed more than touching. She needed to join with him, to become a part of him.

She reached out, closing her hands around the hard length of his desire, and, with a low, rumbling growl, he responded by lifting himself over her. She raised her hips, meeting his thrusting heat with her own sweet burning.

It cost him dearly, his muscles rippling from the effort to hold back, but somehow he managed to enter her slowly. She gasped, holding his arms, but the pain was no more than the tiny flare of a match—brilliant, hot, intense . . . but blessedly brief.

And then, when he again moved within her, there suddenly was nothing but the fire. She cried out her need, and, answering it, he drove into her. Faster, harder, and then faster still, he built the flames, until finally she saw nothing, heard nothing, felt nothing, but the tempestuous roar as they consumed her body, devoured her senses, branded her soul.

She fought for control, but she had no chance of winning. She didn't even want to win. She clung to him as the heat built to a wild, unendurable peak. And then, with one last shuddering cry, she exploded, the flames of her passion gushing high into the cold night sky, lighting it with a liquid shower of a million glowing sparks.

A lifetime later, when they were once again mere mortals capable of normal conversation, light laughter, gentle touches, she lay in his arms. She was so exhausted she could hardly stay awake, and yet so strangely happy she never wanted to sleep again. He stroked her shoulder lightly, smoothing away the sheen of perspiration that still shimmered on her skin.

The fire had burned down to a pile of glowing embers, and now that its light no longer competed, she could see the full moon that rode low in the southern sky, just above the icy treetops.

"Look at the moon," she said sleepily. "Isn't it beautiful?"

She felt him nod. "The mistletoe moon. That's what Alice called it," he said. "We read a story about it once.

It said that if you stood with your true love under the mistletoe moon you would never part.''

At first Lindsay didn't respond, caught unaware by a stab of regret that such pretty stories didn't always come true. Alice and her daddy, who had loved her truly, had stood beneath the mistletoe moon, and still fate had taken her away from him. And very soon…perhaps even tomorrow, Daniel and Lindsay would have to separate, too, each returning to their own lives.

Still, she heard a peace in his voice as he spoke of Alice, a peace that he couldn't have found just a few hours ago. She tried to let that be enough.

''So you see, you were wrong,'' she said softly, reaching up to touch his beard-roughened chin. He hadn't shaved since the power went out two days ago. ''You *do* have some happy memories of Alice.''

She felt him smile under her fingertips. ''Yes, I suppose I do,'' he said, and he bent his head to place a kiss on her hair. ''I have you to thank for that.''

''Any time,'' she said, suffused with a warm, sleepy glow that even common sense wouldn't banish. Not that she had the energy for much common sense. Her sated body needed to rest. Her eyes were heavy, drifting slowly shut. Sleep washed in toward her like waves on an incoming tide.

Perhaps she already was asleep. But when she looked over at the Christmas tree through half-closed lids, she thought she saw its lights flicker and begin to glow. Rich blue, green, red and amber fire, twinkling from the depths of its branches.

She must be dreaming, she thought, but it really didn't matter. Dream or reality, either way it was the most beautiful sight she had ever seen, and she took the miracle of it with her into sleep.

* * *

Daniel knew the instant Lindsay fell asleep. Her sweet body softened, her head relaxing against his arm. He kissed her shoulder, and she didn't even murmur, didn't even stir.

Just at that moment, the power fluttered on. The Christmas tree blazed with a multicolored brilliance. The small red light on his telephone answering machine blinked, then burned steadily. The blue liquid-crystal display of the desk clock began to flash its set of zeros, and somewhere out of the depths of the house, the furnace began to hum.

It was as if, after a period of breathless suspension, the world began again to creak on its axis. And it seemed, somehow, to signal the end of their glorious fantasy. The return to reality.

With a sinking sense of personal failure, Daniel looked down at the poignantly lovely curve of Lindsay's naked hip, so pale and gently rounded, tucked so perfectly up against his own darker and more angular body. He ducked his head into the scented hollow of her neck. Oh, God...what had he done?

But he knew the answer to that. He had used her, plain and simple. She had said that she loved him, and he had used that love to ease a pain that had grown unbearable. But all the while he had know that none of it was real. They had been able to sustain the fantasy only because they were lost in this snowy isolation, in this magical world where there was no time, no place, no other human being to remind them that this kind of thing was madness.

He had warned her, of course. But somehow that warning, issued at the height of her awakening passion, hadn't been quite honest, had it? Deep inside he must have known she'd never turn him away. He had needed her so badly that he had simply taken what he needed and left tomorrow to fend for itself.

Well, tomorrow had arrived. And he still had no idea whether he had committed another grievous sin to add to his list of unforgivable acts, or whether he had blindly reached toward the one woman with whom he had any chance of starting over.

But he could no longer pretend the question wasn't real, wasn't urgent. He gently eased himself around her, settling her sleeping head on a pillow and spreading the blanket over her nakedness. He pulled his own clothes back on swiftly and, walking quietly so that he would not wake her, he went to the desk and called the airport.

The original small plane warnings had been in effect only until 3:00 a.m. His wristwatch said it was already three-thirty. It was time to find out whether the warnings had been extended.

With a start, he realized that, cravenly, he was hoping they had. Perhaps, if the winds were still too high to permit Landwer to bring the helicopter in, Daniel would get a reprieve from the reality he dreaded. Just one more day, he pleaded inwardly. One more day of her warmth, her laughter, her healing touch. *Be honest, McKinley*, he told himself disgustedly. What he really wanted was one day more in her bed, lighting the fire of her amazing passion.

But it was not to be. The warnings had been lifted.

The winds were down to twenty miles per hour, the airport reported. Landwer should have no trouble flying in to pick Lindsay up. If Daniel called his pilot now, Lindsay could easily be home for Christmas.

But, dear God, how could he do it? Though he knew he should, how could he let her go? He shut his eyes, and in his mind he saw her, iridescent as an opal in the abbey's crystal light, flushed with the amber glow of the firelight, silvered by the beams of the mistletoe moon. Fevered by his loving...

He sat there a long, silent moment, his finger on the disconnect button, struggling with his conscience. Then he opened his eyes, and he saw the real Lindsay, sleeping on the sofa, the curve of one bare shoulder visible above the blanket, her face as innocent and trusting as a child.

Suddenly he knew what he had to do. He released the button, heard the hard buzz of the dial tone, and began to punch in Landwer's telephone number.

Lindsay awakened abruptly, aware of the bright daylight streaming in through the picture windows. Almost simultaneously, she realized that Daniel was no longer beside her on the sofa. She looked around the empty room, trying to stay calm, refusing to read his absence as a bad sign. Not yet, anyway, not until she had to. Perhaps he was just in the kitchen, slicing some fresh fruit for their breakfast.

But there were no sounds from the kitchen. There were no sounds at all, in fact. Lindsay sat up, trying to sort out what had happened. Last night, she had become Daniel's lover. That was the simple, strictly factual part. The rest of it was more complicated. Last night, she had been his lover...but what would she be today?

Gradually, as she sat there, she found herself becoming aware of a new, surprising sensation. Warmth. Though she was naked under the blanket, and the fire was burning low in the grate, she was still quite comfortably warm.

She darted a glance toward the Christmas tree, remembering her last vision of it as she fell asleep, alight with burning colors. It had not been a dream, then. The lights were on—the electricity had been restored.

She knew she should be pleased. But, perversely, she found herself longing to return to the frozen darkness in which she and Daniel had clung blindly to each other for warmth and comfort. This morning, with its glaring sunlight and its civilized, artificial warmth, seemed somehow destined to wrench them apart.

Daniel had draped her clothes over the back of the sofa, and, holding the blanket around herself, she awkwardly began to put them on. When she was almost dressed, she called out Daniel's name. But there was no answer.

When, after several minutes, he still had not appeared, she realized it was time to start preparing herself for the worst. He had warned her last night that he was only looking for a temporary fire before which he could warm himself. Yes, he had warned her, and she had promised him it didn't matter.

And it didn't, she assured herself, finding her purse and running a brush through her tangled hair. She had meant what she said. For one night, or for a lifetime, she had wanted to give him whatever he needed. She wasn't going to regret her decision now, just because she had gambled and lost.

She did such a good job with her little peptalk that she didn't even realize how much hope she still cherished in her foolish heart—not until she heard the putter of the incoming helicopter.

No. Please, God, not yet, she wasn't ready to go yet... Still barefoot, she rushed to the window, praying that it wasn't Landwer, praying that it was some other helicopter, coming to take some other woman down some other mountain.

But she would have recognized that big black bird anywhere. It was Landwer. It was Daniel's helicopter. It was coming for her.

Daniel had kept his promise. He had said he'd get her home as soon as possible, and he had let nothing change his plans...certainly nothing as insignificant, she thought, trying not to be bitter, as a little hot love-making by the light of the mistletoe moon.

She found her watch on the floor and, picking it up with trembling fingers, she saw that it was only a little after nine. How efficient he had been! He must have left her arms before the glow had faded from her dreams. He had dried the sweat from his body, donned his clothes again, and gone to the telephone to make his plans to be rid of her.

Her heart cried out a protest, but her mind insisted that she face the facts, however painful they might be. What had really happened here last night? She had told him that she loved him, and he had answered by promising to set her soul on fire. Both of them had been telling no more than the truth.

The helicopter began its descent, whipping the snow from the treetops, creating a mini blizzard in the front yard, and she turned away from the window, searching numbly for her boots. She had to be ready when he called her. She couldn't keep the chopper waiting, not when so many others needed it.

As she sat on the edge of the couch, she glimpsed herself in one of the wall mirrors. How amazing, she thought, turning to stare at the sober-faced young woman in the reflection. She looked exactly as she had when she arrived here four days ago. The same white sweater, a gray skirt, black briefcase. The same long black hair and wide-set blue eyes...nothing, really, to show that her whole world had changed. Nothing to show that when she left this lodge, she would leave her heart behind.

Setting her jaw, she fought the weak tears that threatened to fill her eyes. She mustn't let Daniel see her cry. There must be no more guilt. He had carried far too much for far too long.

The helicopter had set down, and the rotor blades were slowing, allowing the swirling air to settle. Where was Daniel? It was time to say goodbye.

Taking a deep breath, she stood and forced herself to walk to the door. He would come. She knew he would. Still grateful for last night, he would probably give her a particularly tender goodbye kiss. Her stomach clenched. How would she endure it?

As she opened the door, a gust of frigid air ruffled her hair against her neck, and her skirt billowed around her legs. She stared out at the helicopter. Someone was climbing down from the passenger's seat. Bewildered, Lindsay moved to the railing, trying to see who it was.

When it finally fully emerged, the lanky black-clad form was easy to identify, and Lindsay felt a warm rush of affection sweep through her. Roc.

She smiled, ignoring the lump that rose in her throat as she glimpsed the large white bandage over his left temple. How frightened she had been when he fell...and yet his accident had seemed to bring Daniel and Lindsay closer together. They had been forced to put their cold courtesy aside and work together to save him. And it had given Lindsay her first glimpse of the tender side of Daniel...

But she wouldn't think about that now. She would be happy, grateful for this chance to see Roc one more time. She should have known that he would have come to take her place. Roc would not let Daniel sink back into a desolate gloom if he could help it.

Lindsay waved, but Roc had turned back to the helicopter, and, to her amazement, he began pulling out

large, gaily wrapped boxes. They poured out like pieces
of an unassembled rainbow. Two dozen of them, at least,
all tied with bright ribbons of red and green, blue and
silver and gold. Standing there among the growing pile
of gifts, Roc looked a little like a tall, sooty Santa.

Landwer was emerging now, too—and then another
flurry of movement drew Lindsay's eye back to the passenger door. Someone else was getting out... Someone
small and slim, with short dark hair cut in a shiny bob...

Was she dreaming again? It looked like... Suddenly
Lindsay's heart seemed to beat against her throat and,
with a small cry, she began to run, scrambling down the
stairs and hurtling through the snow, ignoring the wind
and the cold. She didn't feel cold. She felt only an intense burst of perfect happiness.

She wasn't dreaming. It was Christy.

Almost two hours later, things had finally settled down.
It had been a madhouse. Lindsay had hugged her sister
amid much incredulous laughter and joyous tears. Daniel
had come out to greet them, charming Christy utterly
with the outrageous comedy act of McKinley and Richter.
Landwer and Roc had carted all the presents into the
house and dumped them under the tree. The pilot had
then returned to the chopper, wrenches in hand, to do
"a little puttering." Daniel had escorted a happily chattering Christy to the guest room. Lindsay had gratefully
taken her first warm shower in two days. Daniel had
been next in line, assuming the hot water held out.

Finally, shooing them all away, Roc had retired to the
kitchen, where he planned, he said, to single-handedly
create a masterpiece for Christmas dinner.

By noon, then, Lindsay was alone in the great room,
arranging the presents carefully under the tree, trying to

believe that any of this was real—and trying to figure out what exactly it all meant.

During the flurry of activity, when she had turned to him with a question in her eyes, Daniel had offered very little explanation. "Well, we already had all the decorations up," was all he would say. "It seemed more efficient to celebrate here." Frustrated, she had appealed to Roc, but he had just smiled, scratching his chin and watching Daniel with a self-satisfied expression.

So she had been given one more day... that was all she could really be sure of. She wanted to believe it meant even more, but she was afraid of the huge, overwhelming need that seemed to leave no room in her chest for any but the shallowest of breaths. So she waited, shifting the packages around again and trying not to hope too hard.

"No peeking, Miss Blaisdell." Daniel's voice came from behind her, and she dropped the package she had been holding, startled. "No presents until after the feast."

"Oh, yes, the McKinley tradition." She turned slowly to face him, trying to remember to breathe. He looked so handsome, fresh-shaven, with his hair still damp from his shower. "Red omelets and green stuffing?"

He smiled. "I think Roc may be able to do a little better than that."

She smiled back. "Better than that? Wow."

But, though the light banter was immensely civilized, she could hardly keep her end up. She felt light-headed at the sight of him, starved for something more meaningful than cocktail party one-liners. *Talk to me, Daniel. Really talk to me*, she wanted to say. *Tell me why you didn't send me home.*

She sighed, unable to speak the words.

"Tired?" He put two fingers under her chin and lifted it, searching her eyes with his piercing blue gaze. She did look tired, she knew. But it wasn't from lack of sleep. It was from worry, and from fear. She had come so close to losing him . . . those helicopter blades had seemed to slice right through her heart.

"A little," she answered, flushing as she remembered how little sleep they had had. Why didn't he look tired, too? He'd been awake far earlier than she had.

He didn't take away his fingers, and he kept studying her face, as if he were trying to decode every shadow, every flicker.

"Tell me something, Lindsay," he said finally. His voice was deep; the note of light teasing had disappeared. "Do you regret what happened last night?"

Even the shallowest breath she took was suddenly painful. "No," she said, meeting his gaze, unflinching.

His eyes darkened. "And the things you said, do you regret them?"

"No," she answered as firmly as her trembling lips would allow. "I love you, Daniel. It may not have been wise to tell you, but I'll never regret doing it."

He inhaled deeply. "I would understand if you did," he said softly. "We were both a little carried away last night. And I know that, at such moments, people tend to use the word 'love' rather freely—"

"You didn't," she said, her voice catching in spite of her attempt to be brave. "You didn't use the word at all."

"I know," he said. "I didn't know what love was then, or whether I could feel it. I'd lived so long with something so different. I didn't want you to come to me believing I could offer you something that I might not ever be able to give you."

Reaching into his pocket, he pulled out a small, square box. It was wrapped in silver paper the color of moonbeams, tied with an opalescent bow that looked as if it had been chipped from the walls of the crystal abbey. She stared at it numbly, much as he had stared at Alice's present last night, afraid to touch it, afraid that it wasn't what she hoped. Perhaps it was her consolation prize, the expensive little apology he offered because he couldn't love her.

"This is for you, Lindsay," he said, lifting her limp hand and pressing the box into it. "Open it."

Her fingers felt weak and clumsy, but somehow she managed to get the box unwrapped. When she hesitated, afraid to lift the lid, afraid to know what lay inside, Daniel reached over and opened it.

"Oh," she said stupidly. "Oh, Daniel." It was the most beautiful ring she had ever seen, a perfect diamond solitaire surrounded by a wreath of alternating rubies and emeralds, which flashed in the sunlight like the Christmas lights she had thought were just a dream.

She felt her eyes welling up with the emotion she'd been holding back all morning. She lifted her gaze to his, letting the warm, wet tears find their way down her cheeks.

"I'm using the word now," he said, his voice husky and deep. "I love you, Lindsay. I think perhaps I've loved you ever since the first day you arrived. You were so cold and angry, and yet so beautiful, so full of life. But I didn't understand what I was feeling—I wasn't really sure, not even after last night. I thought it might be lust or pity or loneliness. Or even some need so desperate it didn't have a name."

He touched her cheek. "But then this morning, while you were sleeping, I called the airport, and they told me that the helicopter was free to fly again. At that moment, when I realized I really was going to lose you, I knew I couldn't live without you. I knew it was love.''

She couldn't speak. Her mind had forgotten all the words it once knew.

He took the ring from the box and slowly slipped it onto her finger. "Marry me," he said, holding her hand in his tightly. "We'll be a family, the three of us. You can teach me how to do it right, just as you've taught me how to love.''

She stared at her hand, looking at the extraordinary ring with a stunned amazement. Impatient, he pulled her around to the side of the tree, where they were half hidden by the branches. He swept her into his arms, his embrace firm and possessive.

"Say it, Lindsay." He spoke with his lips against her hair. The scent of pine floated all around them, cocooning them in its musty scent. "Say yes, before I lose my mind.''

"Yes," she breathed. There seemed to be no other word in her vocabulary. This was the best word. The perfect word. "Yes.''

Daniel bent his head, his lips claiming hers in a kiss that echoed last night's fire. She felt her knees go weak, and she wrapped her arms around his neck for stability.

Suddenly a huge, dark shadow fell across the tree.

With a low curse, Daniel lifted his head, and Lindsay followed suit. Roc stood just five feet away, a turkey baster in his good hand, his hook pointed accusingly at the two of them. Behind him, Christy and Landwer were watching, politely hiding what sounded suspiciously like giggles.

"All right, in there," he said. "That's quite enough of that disgusting mooning and smooching.''

"Go away, Roc," Daniel said. He turned his attention back to Lindsay, pulling her into his embrace.

Roc harrumphed, appealing to Christy with a gesture of helpless frustration.

"Did you hear that? Well, I guess you better know right now, Miss Christy, that Danny Boy McKinley over there, soon to be your brother-in-law, is a serious pain in the posterior. Why, just two days ago, when I was busting my head open trying to get a little flapdoodle going between those two, Danny Boy wouldn't get close enough to your sister to hand her the salt."

He aimed the baster at Daniel like a sword. "Now look at him! Now, when I want the man to come and eat his Christmas dinner, he can't take his grimy paws off her."

"Go away, Roc," Daniel said again, still holding Lindsay, staring down at her lips. "We're busy."

Roc huffed noisily, but, peeking through the branches of the tree, Lindsay was quite sure she saw a twinkle in his eye.

"Come on then, Miss Christy. They'll be out soon enough when they get a sniff of dinner. Romeo would have jumped straight down off Miss Juliet's balcony for a taste of Roc Richter's Christmas turkey."

Christy giggled, casting just one curious look over her shoulder as she left the room in Roc's wake, heading toward the kitchen. Lindsay smiled—this was happier than she had seen Christy be in a long time. The kid was obviously perfectly content to trail after her newfound friend.

"Now," Daniel said, situating Lindsay more comfortably in his embrace. "Where were we?"

"I think," she said, lifting her face toward his expectantly, "that you were about to give me my Christmas present."

HARLEQUIN PRESENTS®

Whose baby?

JACK'S BABY
by
Emma Darcy

Was Nina expecting Jack Gulliver's baby? Jack
hoped so, because he still loved Nina and this could
be his chance to get her back. But he still had to
convince her that one cry from baby Charlotte
wouldn't have him running for the door...!

Available in January wherever
Harlequin books are sold.

Look us up on-line at: http://www.romance.net

TAUTH16

FORBIDDEN!

It shouldn't have been allowed to happen—
but it did!

#1859 *THE MORNING AFTER*
by
Michelle Reid

César DeSanquez believed that supermodel Annie was a
hard-hearted woman who had torn apart his family in the
space of a night. Now, in the cold light of dawn, César
wanted his own back!

Available next month wherever
Harlequin books are sold.

Look us up on-line at: http://www.romance.net

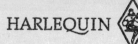 HARLEQUIN 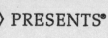 PRESENTS®